THE HEROIC
SURGEON

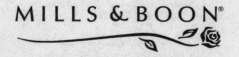

MILLS & BOON®

All the characters in this book have no existence outside the imagination of the author, and have no relation whatsoever to anyone bearing the same name or names. They are not even distantly inspired by any individual known or unknown to the author, and all the incidents are pure invention.

MILLS & BOON and MILLS & BOON with the Rose Device are registered trademarks of the publisher.

First published in Great Britain 2005
Harlequin Mills & Boon Limited,
Eton House, 18-24 Paradise Road, Richmond, Surrey TW9 1SR

© Olivia Gates 2005

ISBN 0 263 84338 6

Set in Times Roman 10½ on 12 pt.
03-1005-47486

Printed and bound in Spain
by Litografia Rosés, S.A., Barcelona

CHAPTER ONE

THE man looked good enough to eat.

Gulnar forced her lids to open wider and her focus to lock and steady. The man didn't disappear. He *was* really here.

His every unhurried step was eloquent with calm authority, every line of his formidably proportioned body with controlled, fluid power. He was a graceful, gorgeous being, even if his clothes hung a bit from the expanse of his impressive shoulders and his uncompromising face was too raw-boned. In fact, the asceticism only added to his impact.

She huffed an incredulous exhalation. Had her mind finally disintegrated with starvation and heat exhaustion?

That man was a murderer. A *terrorist*!

And he was preceding six more terrorists across the municipal building's main hall, towering a whole head over the tallest among them. But he was on a far higher level from his henchmen in every other respect. An Olympian among orang-utans.

She clamped her bone-dry lips, exerted all she had left on steadying her quivering muscles as his head turned this way and that, his hewn face exhibiting no reaction, his eyes sweeping the crowd, sparing no one a lingering look.

Look at me! she heard a voice yelling, and for a moment shriveled in horror that it was hers. It was. But only inside her head. *Get a grip, Gulnar.* She should be praying he wouldn't notice her. God only knew what he'd do if he did!

In the next second she lost whatever control she had on her long-frayed nerves. He was heading towards her!

The heart that had long decelerated into the sluggish rhythm of resignation zoomed behind her ribs, the transition so sudden she felt her grip on consciousness softening…

But the man stopped a few feet away, by the group of people she'd just left, where Mikhael, her last remaining gravely injured casualty, was. His terrorists fanned out, protecting his back, his height keeping him visible above their tight grid.

Fury burst in her chest, cascaded throughout her body. How could she have thought him anything else but a bully, coming in here surrounded by his henchmen, terrorizing the already bludgeoned and broken people? He probably looked good enough to eat because she was hungry enough to eat a rat!

Which she'd probably resort to before long. She wouldn't have to worry about finding one. Rats were becoming braver as the huddled masses grew still and squalor soared. She'd woken up from her shallow slumber at dawn when one had scampered across her chest. Good thing rats didn't faze her. Not much could. Not any more. She was destined to live—and live. And lose. Being held hostage was just one more thing to survive.

And she'd been held hostage with over four hundred people since the militants had erupted into the building three days ago, in a storm of gunfire and thundering threats on the public address system. The place was rigged with explosives. They would shoot anyone who moved.

What had followed had been total pandemonium.

When the gunfire had stopped there had been thirty-two people down.

The only hostage with medical experience, overwhelmed and unequipped, she'd raced among the casualties, trying to set up some form of triage, some measure of emergency intervention.

Some had been killed outright, some had had injuries beyond the help of her improvised measures. But the ones who'd ruptured her heart with loss and futility had been those whose injuries would have been controllable had she had access to even the most basic emergency supplies. But there were none, and she'd lost eleven of the injured she was tending. Mikhael was the only one she hadn't lost. Yet. It was a matter of time, and the ones with lesser injuries would follow.

She'd tried to talk reason to the only woman militant, pleaded for the injured to be turned over to the security forces who now besieged the building. It was one thing to kill people in the heat of the moment, another to let them die such slow, agonizing deaths. They'd still have hundreds under their power to bargain with.

Nothing had worked. No concessions would be offered before the militants' demands were met. Gulnar had almost laughed in the woman's face, could have told her how this would end.

Hostage situations often ended with everyone losing and everything far worse than before, the ever-expanding shockwaves of retaliation and counter-retaliation only creating new generations raised on oppression, hatred and intolerance, perpetuating the vicious circle of violence, strife and death.

Her mind was wrenched back to the moment as one of the man's henchmen handed him a suitcase. No, that looked like…a huge emergency bag? He kneeled on the floor, opened it and—*it was*!

What did that mean? Were there reporters around? And were the militants putting on a show of mercy for their benefit?

So what? The man had an emergency bag and that was all that mattered. All she needed.

Brutal hope tore aside her remaining tatters of self-preservation, propelled her to her feet. A burning torrent of pins and needles almost sent her to the floor again. They hadn't been letting them up to even go to the bathroom.

Ignoring the debilitating electricity, she limped over to the man, her hands raised in the universal gesture of surrender. "Please, let me use the emergency supplies!"

One of the militants' gazes swept over her, rabid, defiling. "Sit down now!"

She wasn't going to sit down! She was getting her hands on those supplies. He could do what he liked.

And what he liked, and so much, was to show her who was boss. He rammed the butt of his semi-automatic rifle into her shoulder, hard. Too hard. She heard a sickening crack. In the flash before pain exploded from her shoulder to flood her body she wondered—had he dislocated it? Broken it? Could she manage with one arm?

Then the impact was transmitted to the rest of her. Just before she launched backwards in the air, feeling weightless, powerless, the man with the emergency bag turned around and his gaze lodged on her across the distance and everything stopped. For a second. An hour. Then she slammed to the ground. Head first. Her body followed, the impact driving her bones into her flesh.

All air left her lungs and blackness swelled, overflowed from all sides.

Great, just great. The bitter thought burst on and off in her flickering mind. She'd pass out, leaving that man to muck about playing doctor, probably finishing Mikhael off!

So it was simple. She wouldn't pass out. It didn't matter that she was starving and dying of thirst, that she'd banged her head on the marble floor. Passing out wasn't an option.

She growled at the pain and resignation telling her to let go. For an eternity, the harder she struggled the faster she sank. Then a sound permeated the inky molasses filling her head. A comforting sound. ''Shh, shh.''

Her mind finally registered what her eyes were staring at. The man. It was him who was soothing her.

She jackknifed to a sitting position and his hands, firm but gentle on her arms, slackened. She gaped at him.

Close up, he really was flawless. And those eyes slammed into her with more force for being so near. Beautiful. Hypnotic. Intense white on endless black. Cool with secret power, remote as if he existed in this plane only in image. Yet intense with—what? Anger? Annoyance? No—it felt like worry. Mercy…

She must have had a concussion if she was picking up such potent, pure signals where they didn't exist.

But, no. Concussion or not, she read people. Fathomed them. Had yet to be wrong. These eyes, this face, this aura—these were the products of a lifetime well spent, the reflection of an untarnished soul. This was no extremist who fought his fanatic battles by murdering innocent civilians.

Or she could be letting his staggering looks or her

own blinding pain get to her. Whatever the truth was, she had to obtain a promise of his mercy. For her casualties. For Mikhael.

She struggled to her knees, knocking his hands away, her own clawing at his arms. These tensed to cabled steel beneath her grip. "Sir, please! You have to let me use the medical supplies! I am a nurse and I could save those people."

A frown answered her outburst then his lips clamped on an exasperated sigh. He shook his head and reached for hers.

It took all her will not to shout what the hell he thought he was doing. *Don't antagonize him.* She stifled her objections, sat motionless as long, careful fingers probed her skull, sculptor-like. Palpating for bumps? It seemed he'd found them for his frown grew even blacker.

He rose, his hands on her shoulder keeping her firmly down. He silently pointed his forefinger at her, shook it once, his message clear. Stay there.

"I can't stay here! I have to help. Please!"

His headshake was accompanied by eye-rolling this time. He rubbed his eyes, leveled them on her, his expression tinged with…bewilderment? He couldn't believe one of his victims wasn't afraid of him. And to think she'd felt compassion coming off him in waves!

He dismissed her again and turned to open the bag. She lunged for a saline bag, but he snatched it away and held it out of her reach. In the next second he dropped it in utmost surprise when she struck his hand with all her strength. His men advanced but he waved them away. He shook his head, looked her square in the eyes, his expression unmistakable this time. Total disgusted resignation.

He sighed. "I get your rage lady, just not why you're aiming it at me. You're making those guys so twitchy they may open fire just to shut you up. How can I explain that to you, and that this saline bag isn't drinking water, when you don't speak a word of English and I don't speak your language?

Dante couldn't believe the woman had finally stopped fighting him. Her mouth had dropped open and remained that way. Score one for the magical powers of his soothing tones.

Nah. She'd probably just depleted herself. Or maybe concussion was setting in. Maybe it had all been the concussion talking.

A shudder spiraled through him again. That bang her head had made on the floor still pounded in his ears, still vibrated up his bones. It was a miracle she hadn't passed out. Her head must be tougher that it looked.

And it looked good. Too good. Even smothered in that garish headscarf. His own scarf looked worse, dirty and tattered, but he'd made do with anything he'd found when he'd lost his own.

It was amazing. Not that she still looked stunning after days of terror and starvation and abuse, but that he'd noticed it now. That it affected him this way.

Oh, all right. He'd be dead if he didn't. If it didn't. And against common belief, including his own, it seemed he wasn't after all. What a time to discover he was still alive.

It was probably just an illusion. And, anyway, *staying* alive wasn't high on his priority list. That had brought him to these parts of the world, had gotten him past those madmen. His one and only priority now was keeping that man alive.

He turned to his emergency bag, extracted what he'd need for first-line measures of resuscitation. Ringer's lactate bags, IV lines, cannulae, syringes, plastic bags for blood collection…

"What did you say?"

Dante started. English. Clear, American-accented English. The last thing he'd ever thought to hear here. And from her.

He snapped his eyes up, found her lips hanging open. OK. He had needed communication with a fellow human being for too long, finding local languages too hard to grasp, that he was starting to hear things.

He resumed his task, got out sealed, pre-sterilized scissors, clamps, scalpels…

"What am I saying? I know what you said!" There she went again! Speaking in almost accent-free English, in those same hot-caress tones. "But you're speaking English. Why? How?"

It had only been thirty-six hours since he'd last eaten. He couldn't be hallucinating with hypoglycemia already, could he? He looked at her again, into those incredible green irises. "Why and how yourself? And so well? Even the highest officials here speak such broken English I haven't been able to explain my business with the militants or anything else. Beyond flashing my Global Aid Organization credentials…"

"*You're* with *GAO*?" She couldn't have been more incredulous if he'd said he was with the fairy godmother.

"Yeah. Any problems with that?"

Full, dimpled lips thinned into a wrathful line. "Yeah, just one. You're lying. I've been with GAO in this region for seven years, and I've never seen you!"

"So you've seen every GAO operative in the Caucasus?"

"What's your name?"

He blinked at her imperative tone. His lips twitched. "Dante Guerriero, at your service."

Auburn eyebrows rose. "Never heard of you either. And I've at least *heard* of everyone of theirs here. There aren't that many international operatives in the area—as anyone knows who's really with GAO."

His patience was running out fast. She was keeping him from his job, dammit. "If *you* were really with GAO, you'd know nothing matters but the victims."

"Exactly. So if you'll just let me tend to them…?"

He ignored her, spread out his instruments on a layer of sterile gauze. He stopped her again from reaching for gloves, put them on himself, and she blurted out, "Why don't you flash me your GAO credentials?"

"Why should I? Neither GAO nor the Azernian officials told me they have an operative on the inside I had to report to. Tell you what, why don't you go sit in your corner again, nurse your concussion and I'll take care of that man here?"

"His name is Mikhael! I've already lost too many people and I'm damned if I'm going to lose him now, too—when I don't have to."

"You won't lose him. Not if I have anything to say about it."

"Besides having GAO's emergency supplies, what are your qualifications? If you've just joined GAO, you must be new to the field, but I'm a surgical and emergency nurse trained extensively in field injuries and mass casualty situations—"

"And I'm a trauma and reconstructive surgeon." That silenced her, thank God. "And since I've probably been putting people back together since you were in middle school, that makes me the triage officer in charge here.''

Those unbelievable eyes flashed every shade of green, with—what? Hope? More suspicion? From her next words, both, it seemed. ''You're a surgeon?''

He gave his mismatched, miserable garments a cursory grimace. ''I admit I don't look the part.'' He couldn't remember the last time he'd worn the trappings of his profession. He turned his focus to appraising her appearance. Not a good idea. There was no way he could give her neutral scrutiny. He cleared his throat. ''But, then, I've got nothing on you. Let's just agree we're not catching each other at our best, hmm?''

''Are you telling me the truth?''

His gaze moved heavenwards. He exhaled. ''You have a name?''

She blinked at his sudden twist in subject. ''Gulnar.''

A name as laden with sensuality as its bearer. Which was a ridiculous thing to note in their circumstances. ''Gulnar, cross my heart, I'm a surgeon. So if you are really a nurse…''

''If? Look closely, Dr. Gur—Gue—Dr. Dante!'' She pointed at Mikhael. ''You think this is the handiwork of his fellow clerks?''

A closer look validated her point. Mikhael had abdominal and upper-thigh gunshot wounds. And he was still alive after three days. The pressure bandages on his upper thigh were highly professional, ingenious even, made from clothes donated by others. Not soaked through, indicating they'd been applied with pressure adequate enough to stop his hemorrhage, yet not too much to block venous blood return and cause gangrene. An even more creative splint kept his leg immobile, guarding against compounding the injury, and extended, guarding against muscle contracture. The blood flow from his abdominal wound had been as meticulously stemmed. She'd definitely saved the man's life and limb so far.

He nodded his concession, yet couldn't resist making a point of his own. "See how annoying it is to have your credentials and intentions disputed? When you're risking a bullet in the head every moment to get your job done?"

Peach invaded her wraithlike pallor, cascaded from high cheekbones down her neck. Then lower. To that narrow strip of taut, glistening flesh between the two undone buttons of her long-sleeved khaki shirt...

Why was she still smothered in it anyway? She must have left Mikhael's clothes on to guard against the hypothermia associated with shock and blood loss. But almost everyone else was down to their underwear to minimize sweating in the stifling heat, warding off inevitable dehydration. Not that it was working. Most people had already collapsed. But not Gulnar. He wondered what kept her going. What kept her shirt on. Not that keeping it on reduced her effect on him.

Without another look at her, he assembled his laryngoscope and picked an endotracheal tube. She fidgeted. May as well give her something to do. Without looking at her, he said, "Assess circulation, gain venous access and start fluid replacement while I intubate him. Just a liter to boost his blood volume and improve his blood pressure. Too much fluid after such blood loss isn't advisable because—"

She interrupted him. "Because it would dilute his blood and coagulation factors, leading to acidosis, hy-

pothermia and coagulation failure. Death by over-
zealous resuscitation.''

All right. Score one for her emergency medicine
knowledge. She was for real, then.

She finished recording blood pressure. "Eighty over
fifty. But since his shock isn't due only to hemorrhage
but also to dehydration, his remaining blood must be
concentrated. In the absence of blood volume booster
alternatives I don't think we can afford *not* to give him
more fluids.''

So not only for real, but real good, too. And absolutely right. But he did have an alternative. "I would've
recommended far less fluid to start with if I hadn't taken
that into account. A liter is enough. He needs whole
blood after that.''

"Whole blood? Where will we get that?''

"From me.'' Her slanting eyes rounded. He elabo-
rated. "I'm O-negative, the universal donor. And you'll
come in handy here. Better you than me drawing my
own blood one-handedly. But first I'll secure Mikhael's
airway and breathing.''

He moved towards the woman holding Mikhael's
head in her lap, tried to replace her—but the woman
was having none of it. His soothing didn't work this
time. His glance darted towards Gulnar. "What did I
do this time?''

Gulnar's shrug was sort of apologetic. "I've taught
her to perform a jaw thrust and told her to keep him
like that, that if she didn't he'd suffocate on his
tongue.''

It was only then that he noticed—the woman was
holding Mikhael's jaw thrust forwards. The optimum
position to keep a patent airway.

Gulnar turned to the woman, rapping out rapid

Azernian, her voice riding the exotic intonations, making music of every stress and release in every syllable. It was incredible how she switched between languages like that, how each sounded so authentic, so effortless. So elegant. How many more languages did she know? Did Italian feature among her linguistic talents?

Finally the agitated woman slumped, slithered across the floor to let him replace her at Mikhael's head, and sat a few feet away, whimpering. He raised one eyebrow at Gulnar as he positioned Mikhael's head in his lap.

She sighed. "It took some convincing to make her believe you're not with the militants, that you're a doctor and would take care of Mikhael. I even had to lie a bit."

"What about?"

"I told her your name and she said it sounded Italian and I took advantage of that, lied to boost her trust in you."

"And the lie is?"

"That you're related to the most famous humanitarian international operative the region has known, Lorenzo Banducci."

Now, that was completely unexpected. An incredulous huff escaped him. "Lorenzo! Son of a gun. Is he still around?"

"He left the front line about a year ago." Was that regret filling her sigh? Whatever it was, he didn't like the sound of it. Not one bit. "He's in Africa now, working with and married to Sherazad, a doctor who's worked with us here."

Dante turned his attention on Mikhael as he absorbed this, started suctioning his throat, and was stunned to find it clear. He raised his eyes to her.

She answered his unvoiced question. "I've kept his throat clear of secretions and his airway patent with a straw."

"Very resourceful!" He injected Mikhael with a muscle relaxant in lieu of anesthesia as he was already comatose then introduced a nasogastric tube down his throat and into his stomach, decompressing it and guarding against regurgitation of gastric secretions into the respiratory tract.

"The tube isn't yielding blood," he commented.

"Great. So the stomach and intestines aren't injured."

He nodded, aligned Mikhael's neck, tilted it backwards. "So you've worked with Lorenzo?" Which was the essence of stupidity as questions went, since she'd already said as much.

"Yeah, sixteen months. That's counting the two months during which he'd been abducted."

So she'd kept strict count of the months with and those away from Lorenzo!

Oh, grow up! And say something neutral. "Lorenzo and I crossed paths a few times, swapped a lot of notes, and it was good to let rip in Italian again. But we can't be related. I'm only Italian-American." OK, that didn't sound too neutral. Lorenzo was more than a passing acquaintance. He was a friend, for heaven's sake. It wasn't his fault Gulnar had clearly had an eye for him. And the man wasn't here any more. Happily married, too. He hoped.

Stop it!

He passed the endotracheal tube down Mikhael's trachea, inflated its cuff to secure it against slipping out and started delivering 100 per cent oxygen. He picked his next words more carefully. "Though, come to think of it, we are probably related. My family comes from Florence and all Florentines are related somehow.''

A smile warmed her eyes. ''So I was more of a clair-voyant than a liar.''

Her warmth went right through his chest. ''You can be anything you like as long as you're my translator.''

He inserted a Foley's catheter. No blood came with the urine. He heaved a sigh of relief. No urogenital in-juries either.

With his first measures complete, he allowed his gaze to linger on Gulnar's face, found concentration knotting her elegant eyebrows as she placed the cannula in Mikhael's arm, connected it to the IV line, handed the saline bag to Mikhael's lady friend to hold up, and set the drip to maximum.

Placing the cannula must have been hell. Mikhael's veins were long collapsed and with the way her left arm was pressed to her side—*why* was she holding it like that…?

The realization, the memory hit him. The knock she'd taken! Was her shoulder injured? It must be…

Reach out for her, examine her—enfold her…

He barely stopped his impetuous move towards her, squashed the roiling urge and the end of a tourniquet between clamped teeth. Not a good time. And it never would be either. He was done reaching out. Never again on a personal basis. He'd finish this and move on. And on. He'd sworn it. He'd continue living on the fringes, alone and separate.

He'd die the same way.

CHAPTER TWO

"Now—blood."

Gulnar's eyes swung up at Dante's terse command. He wrapped the tourniquet around his arm and snapped it hard in place, hoping the lash of pain would end his wandering thoughts.

If only it were that easy. He sighed and presented Gulnar with his arm turned upwards, exposing his bulging veins, handed her the line of the blood bag, capped needle first. She hesitated.

He exhaled. "*Now* what?"

She chewed her lower lip. "We can't just do a transfusion without checking your blood. But we *can* give him more fluids and he's more or less stable…"

"Trust me, I'm clean. You can't imagine how clean. And I'm bursting with packed red blood cells and clotting factors."

Gulnar bit into her lip and he exhaled, feeling his arm going cold and numb with the tourniquet's constriction. He could have done without the aggravation. Could have done with Gulnar's help. One more thing he'd have to do without, then.

He reached for the needle and she resisted. His hand fisted in exasperation. Blood hissed in his ears. He snapped another bag up, snatched the cap off its needle with his teeth. "Even if you don't believe me, don't you think it's worth the risk to save Mikhael now? And what possible reason would I have for lying? For infecting him with—what? AIDS, presumably? Aren't you taking this paranoia too far?''

He raised his eyes to flay her with his irritation, met her magnificent eyes and it was he who flinched.

''When you wake up one day, Dr. Dante,'' she snarled, ''and find the neighbors you've lived with all your life have turned into enemies, when they take over your home, make you run for your life, when the people you think will offer you sanctuary kill everyone you know and love, when you've survived fifteen years of war and displacement, it's not very hard to see how one can end up paranoid!''

He gaped at her, his heart constricting, his throat closing.

''From what you described, it's a miracle to only end up paranoid after all that. But, paranoid or not, I will do this with or without your consent. You can help me or you can go back to your corner and stop hindering me.''

At his vehemence something leapt in her eyes, settled there. Something softening, acquiescent. His body lurched, his head tightened. Hell. He'd take her antagonism any day.

His breath eased only when her eyes released him and she took the needle from his fingers.

So she'd decided to trust him, huh? Good to know. Too good. It felt even better to surrender to her ministrations as without another word or glance she slipped the needle into his vein. He didn't even feel it piercing his skin, didn't feel the tourniquet being snapped off. A soothing touch, a perfect approach. He sighed, watched his blood filling the collection bag and handed her one more bag to add to the one she already had.

Her eyes sought his as he pumped his hand. ''Three

bags?'' He nodded. "You can't donate all that blood. Those bags have to be a pint each!''

"Five hundred ccs actually. I'm a big man, I have lots to spare.''

"Excuse me, but you don't look as if you do!''

He couldn't say it surprised him. He wasn't back to normal, and wondered if he ever would be. Normal… It felt like another man's life when normal had even been applicable. But he wasn't thrilled to know she thought so, too. In fact, it chafed. More, even, than Roxanne's revulsion.

A surge of despondency and irritation wouldn't be contained. "Just hook Mikhael to the first unit, give him 400 ccs for now. Save the rest for afterwards. He's bound to lose more blood when I explore his injuries and during definitive repairs. I'll take care of the rest.'' She opened her mouth. His taut words closed it. "Allow me the courtesy of assuming I know my own limits.''

A heartbeat later she hurled back an equally tense rejoinder. "It's against all safety protocols, donating more than 750 ccs of blood! What if—''

"If I'd been shot, I would have lost far more than 1500 ccs, and I wouldn't have had the luxury of re-placing the blood volume, like I will now.''

"But Mikhael may not need all that blood!''

"If Mikhael doesn't need it, someone else will.''

Her grudging concession was in her every move as she unhooked the blood bag from his needle and hooked it to Mikhael's cannula, her motions precise with sup-pressed annoyance and resignation.

He hooked the second blood bag on. Fumbled it on, more like. Something warm and weakening was seeping through his limbs, shooting his co-ordination to hell. He could deal with everything. Danger, violence, madness.

Desperation, terror, agony. But not what Gulnar was offering him now. Caring.

No one had cared what happened to him in a very long time.

Hah! No one had ever cared what happened to him.

He'd been taught that indelible lesson six years ago, when the illusion of being a needed part of a relationship—a family—had been eradicated. When he'd stopped fooling himself into thinking he counted beyond what he could provide.

But Gulnar was showing him he did. As another human being only, sure, but she still did care. About a stranger, someone she'd just met. Just on principle. She was taking it very hard, the idea of endangering him, even to save the young man she was torn up over.

And her caring hurt him, breached his defences. He couldn't afford that now.

Forget her. Forget yourself. Get this done.

Still clenching and unclenching his left fist to help the blood flow, he turned to Mikhael, reassessed his vitals. His pulse was slowing down, his breathing deepening. Good. Their measures were stabilizing his general condition. On to his specific injuries.

Dante undid the abdominal bandages, noted no renewed bleeding from the two entry wounds. He raised his eyes to Gulnar who had finished delivering the blood and rechecking Mikhael's blood pressure.

She answered the question in his eye. ''BP 100 over 70.''

Her whisper raised goose-bumps all over his body. She was dimming. But she'd carry on until she was extinguished. He knew nothing about her, yet he knew this, knew the lengths she'd go to for others.

He checked her pulse. Fast. Thready. He must do something about it, now!

She moved out of his reach, darting glances towards their captors. He'd totally forgotten about them.

About everyone.

The captives had slumped back into their despair now they'd understood who he was, how his presence would probably mean nothing to most of them. The militants had turned their backs on them, the occasional looks over their shoulders expressing how bored they were with it all, how they hated escorting him in to save even one enemy. But they had their orders.

"*You* need resuscitation."

She shrugged. "Not more than any other uninjured person here."

"But *you* are expected to help me. You're no use to me if you faint. Just one liter of saline…"

She cut him off. "May mean life for one of the injured people. I'll go give them blood and fluids." She rose and moved away before he could say anthing else.

Dante turned to Mikhael, gave his wounds another careful palpation. He knew the bullets hadn't caused much damage here. He'd finished a full exam by the time she'd got back.

She sank to her knees beside him, checked Mikhael's BP again. "Holding. So—what do you think? Mikhael's blood pressure is a strong indication there's no ongoing intra-abdominal bleeding."

He nodded. "Whatever blood loss he suffered from the abdominal wounds was hepatic in origin."

Gulnar wiped the back of her forearm across her forehead, soaking her sleeve with more precious moisture. "I thought as much. The damage was to the tail of the liver's right lobe. If the bullets had hit its blood vessels network, I doubt he would have lasted an hour.''

"It's a relief. I wasn't looking forward to performing a laparotomy under septic conditions. There's nothing more I should do, at the moment, about his abdominal injuries, now that bleeding has stopped.''

Gulnar nodded and began cleaning the wounds. He helped her wrap the man's abdomen in bandages again, and found himself asking, ''I know the main info from the news and the officials. But I want you to tell me what happened here, in detail.''

She looked at him, her eyes impassive. ''You see the result. What good are details?''

He didn't know why he was asking either. He just needed to know. Then something else occurred to him. ''If you'd rather not repeat what happened, relive—''

"It's not that! It's just…'' She hesitated for one more second. Then she told him. All the details of the raid, the indiscriminate killings, the monstrous treatment afterwards.

He shouldn't have asked.

But it blasted everything into perspective, made whatever he'd thought he'd suffered insignificant.

And made whatever he did pointless?

No. What he did couldn't be pointless. He had to make it count. One life at a time snatched out of the jaws of death and cruelty. One lesser defeat, one less than total disaster.

He had to believe that. He had to.

It was all he lived for.

Gulnar closed her eyes against the sunlight slanting through the building's high windows. Against Dante's searing turmoil. There was no shying away from his frustration, his rage. Somehow, sharing distress with him halved it this time, as if he was absorbing it, diffusing it.

She opened her eyes and saw him in control again, removing the pressure bandages around the top of Mikhael's thigh.

She clung to his hand. "If he's stabilizing now, shouldn't we just inject him with a massive dose of antibiotics, give him a tetanus booster and monitor him?"

Those eyes still crackled with aggression, unmeant for her yet still daunting. They ignored her and her protest, turned to his task. Her eyes followed his exploration. Her stomach quivered at the fist-sized wound blasted in Mikhael's thigh. Handling it in the heat of the moment, bathing in his blood, she hadn't had awareness enough to dwell on the horror. Three days since it had happened, it looked far worse. How bad did Dante think it was?

Whatever his diagnosis, his lips twisted on it. He reapplied a fresh pressure bandage, announced his verdict. "I have to tend to his vascular injury now or he will lose his leg even if we save his life."

"Oh." A flash of agony seared her. "I guess I put off thoughts of complications and prognoses, knowing there was nothing I could do about them."

"It's lucky his leg isn't gangrenous by now. But there's a lot of damage to his common femoral artery and vein."

Every catastrophic complication reared its head now she'd let herself think. "But if there is the slightest chance intervention could dislodge a clot and cause an embolism, shouldn't we choose between life and limb?"

"No."

Just no? "Care to elaborate?"

Evidently not. He started spreading his surgical instruments on a pre-sterilized surgical towel. She tried again. "What *can* you do here?"

"I've done vascular repair in worse conditions."

Her eyes darted to the filthy floor, the limited instruments. "*Worse* conditions?"

"A trench with raining shrapnel, with your operating arm almost out of order are worse conditions, don't you think?"

She had to agree.

He continued. "And I didn't have a grade-A surgical nurse to assist me then." He turned away, produced disposable surgical drapes, large swabs and a bottle of povidone-iodine. "Help yourself. I need both his legs prepped down to his feet."

It took her only seconds to comply, all the time hearing Mikhael's lover's rising sobs. Seeing her man reduced to a draped body, with only the field of surgery exposed, must be adding to her indelible trauma.

Dante's authoritative voice snatched her attention back to where it counted. "Top up the muscle relaxant, and inject 10 milligrams of morphine direct into the cannula. That will have to do for anesthesia."

He waited for her to finish then made his first incision three inches above the site of injury, exposing the external iliac artery. "Here's where I deal with your clot worries. I'll occlude the vessels above and below the site of injury, so that a hemorrhage doesn't obscure the operating field. And the clot will have nowhere to go. Clamp!"

She handed him a non-crushing vascular clamp, watched him applying it gently to the artery. "Why

didn't you use slings?'' She'd learned from experience
that a special surgical shoelace-like string passed twice
around an artery was the best way to occlude it.

He answered without raising his eyes from his task.
''A sling may be the method of choice with every other
artery, but not the aorta or iliac arteries. There's too
much risk of injuring the lumbar and iliac veins.''

She hadn't known that.

''It's incredible that you know about slings in the first
place. Most schools of thought advocate non-crushing
clamping as the only method of vessel occulsion.'' Was
he letting her off the hook after she'd boasted of her
vast experience in trauma medicine? No, it had sounded
like praise.

Heat rose inside her. Embarrassment? Gratitude?
More? Whatever it was, it spread in places long un-
touched, believed untouchable, dead...

Dante was now incising the skin three inches below
the site of injury, exposing the continuation of the femoral artery. This time he took the sling she handed him,
wound it twice around the artery.

With hemorrhage and clot control now assured, she
undid the bandages for him, anticipating his need.

His lips tugged. ''Thanks. On to debriding the
wound.'' Now he'd dealt with the haemorrhage it was
time to clean the wound.

Without him asking for it, she placed two self-
retaining retractors strategically to open the surgical
field. This time he didn't thank her, but she felt his
approval. She couldn't remember the last time anything
had felt so good.

A tap on the back of her hand attracted her attention.
''See this? Vein is hanging by a thread and artery is

transected. We're very lucky it got severed below the origin of the collateral branch.''

A closer look showed both ends of the severed femoral artery had recoiled into the surrounding tissues. Dante dissected extensively to find the edges. ''Do you think you will need to graft?'' she asked.

He exhaled, pulled on one edge. ''The vein can be directly sutured, thank God. As for the artery, that depends. If there has been too much tissue loss, or if I have to cut enough tissue that the ends won't meet without tension, I'll have to have a graft.''

Attached under tension, the reattached artery would die and probably cause gangrene or even a fatal hemorrhage.

Minutes later he sighed. ''No use. Let's harvest that graft.''

She nodded, swooped to inject both ends with saline to assess the potency of the artery and the vein, then reported. ''Return rate indicates an extensive thrombus formation. Do you have a Fogarty catheter?''

He pointed without raising his head, picking a scalpel. ''It's with the other catheters.''

In seconds she'd cleared both ends of vein and artery of clotted blood. ''Shall I flush it out with heparinized saline?''

That brought his eyes up and something like a smile to them. ''Remind me to thank every mentor you've ever had, Gulnar.''

She glowed with pride. It wasn't a sane reaction, but an unstoppable one.

He'd already moved to Mikhael's other leg, made an incision at the groin identifying the greater saphenous vein. He began harvesting it through an incision over the course of the vein. He stopped at the inner knee. ''I will need only this much. No need to extend the incision into the calf,'' he explained.

After exposure of the required length of vein, he deepened his dissection then looked at her. ''Need your help here, if you're done.'' She nodded eagerly. ''Mix me 120 milligrams papaverine in 250 ccs Ringer's.''

For a few seconds she couldn't see where the papaverine was in the bag. Then she spotted it, snapped it up, but still couldn't understand what he needed it for. *Just hand the man what he asked for.*

She did, just as he explained. ''I'll irrigate the vein with it, to prevent spasm and to distend it to a suitable size for grafting with the wider femoral artery.''

He then tied the major tributaries of the vein and cut them. Once he'd removed the vein segment embedded in surrounding tissue, he prepared it further for grafting.

After he'd examined the graft segment and deemed it dilated enough, he grafted it in place.

Throughout the delicate procedure, it was as if she'd always worked with him. She anticipated his demands, handing him materials, providing him with better access, swabbing blood, cutting sutures just as close or as far as he needed.

Satisfaction flooded her, as unlikely as it was in their conditions. But she couldn't help savoring it. There was nothing better in life, nothing more worthwhile, than being part of the restoration of another human being. And Dante was indeed a miracle worker. She'd only ever seen one surgeon who possessed such speed, such unerring, almost prophetic skill. Lorenzo. Still, Dante had something over him, an artistic quality to his every move, a gentle, esthetic flair that went beyond precision, was above uncanny skill. This was talent.

He put the last suture into the arterial repair and exhaled. "What I wouldn't have given for intra-operative angiography. But I guess we'll just to believe you've cleared all the clots and prevented re-formation."

She prayed so, and saw as fierce a hope in his eyes. She wasn't up to facing such intensity now. She looked away, examined Mikhael's leg. Her heart thumped. "His leg is swelling. Could he develop compartment syndrome now?" This which would cut off the blood flow and cause gangrene!

He nodded.

Without another word she handed him instruments and he performed a fasciotomy, cutting bone-deep through the thigh separating its compartments, the only way to relieve the build-up of pressure there.

He sighed when he was done. "I'm not happy I added more trauma, increasing risk of infection, but the alternative—"

She shuddered and administered the highest possible dose of antibiotics and tetanus toxoid, then rechecked Mikhael's leg. Though it looked horrifying, she knew Dante had managed to save it. There would be scarring, but Mikhael would walk on it, probably run again. If they survived this.

She was applying a dressing to the limb when Dante made a strange sound. She raised her eyes, sought his. She didn't find them. Just blank whites staring back at her. Then his lids slammed shut just before he slumped to the floor.

CHAPTER THREE

"DANTE! Dante!"

A shrill sound slashed through the darkness. Something shook his immovable body. He wanted to make it stop, to leave him alone in the dark. He couldn't. He had no voice. No muscles. He should be worried, but he wasn't. Then it wasn't dark any more, but a painful red burning on the backs of his eyelids.

Suddenly it dimmed and he ventured to open his eyes. He stared into forest-lush green. Eyes. Gulnar's. That was her name. The woman who belonged in dreams. In abandoned fantasies. What was she doing in this nightmare?

Now she was pouncing on him, stinging him. He heard a protest. His. "Ow. That hurt…"

He remembered snatches of…surgery? A vascular repair, a fasciotomy… Had he finished? Yes—yes, he guessed so. The last thing he recalled was watching dainty hands in surgical gloves wrapping Vaseline gauze around a mutilated limb, then there were flashes of blue and purple and intense, nauseating yellow. Then everything blinked out.

He'd fainted.

She'd been right. He didn't have enough blood to spare. Pathetic. Just a liter and a half of blood and his system had shut down. They'd forgotten to initiate his fluid replacement, had gotten sidetracked tending to Mikhael. And he'd lectured her about not being of any use to him if she fainted!

Now she was rectifying their oversight. His arm throbbed where she'd shoved the cannula without any finesse this time. She hooked it to the line of the Ringer's solution bag.

She heaved herself up to her feet to hold the bag up so the fluid would flow—and staggered. She would have fallen if he hadn't somehow summoned enough strength and co-ordination to get to his feet and catch her.

She was limp, shaking like a leaf. It had to be from starvation and dehydration. Concussion. But what if it was more? What if an artery had ruptured inside her head? What if all that life, all that beauty was being snuffed as he watched, helpless, useless? Like he would watch all those others…

He heard her gasped words from a long, narrowing tunnel of panic. "Stood up too suddenly, got light-headed…"

He tightened his arms around her when she swayed again.

"And postural hypotension is becoming the constrictive type now."

What?

"You're cutting off my circulation."

His frantic gaze swept her incredible face. Was she joking?

She was!

So was she OK? Dared he relax?

Dante pushed Gulnar down beside the emergency bag. "I'm examining you. And you're getting fluid replacement, too, whether you agree or not."

"Yes, Doctor."

He couldn't believe it. She was teasing him. And he wanted to whoop with laughter. He must have snapped. She must have, too, long before him.

He shone a penlight into her eyes. Good. Equal, brisk pupillary reflexes. No cupping of the optic disc, no hazing of the retina. Normal fundus, if a little pale. That had to do with her dehydration. Probably anemic, too.

But no brain swelling. Her reflexes were all fine. OK. No detectable sequels to the blow. On to fluid replacement.

Ready with a cannula, he pushed up her sleeve, revealed her creamy, supple forearm.

Hell! What was wrong with him when, in a situation as dire as this, all he wanted was to close those eyes and open those lips, taste her, drown in her life, drain all horror and desperation in her passion and compassion?

It was probably a stress reaction. That made no difference to its impact. Probably intensified it. After his accustomed apathy it was jarring to experience such searing urgency again. Again? Had he ever felt anything like that?

Not that he remembered.

He inserted the cannula, hooked the line, watched the fluid coursing through it and into her, willed it to revive her. He would die, and more, to see her safe, saved.

The most wonderful sound tickled him. Her giggle. "You have to admit, we look ridiculous, each hooked to a line and holding the other's bag up."

"We do look like broken-down machines in Maintenance."

"We are."

"You're right. But what else are you? You're not Azernian or Badovnan. And though your English is near perfect, it isn't your mother tongue, is it? Right now I can't access my geography and history, can't think which country has been in a fifteen-year war and whose people have been displaced."

She caressed an apology to the darkening stain where she'd shoved his cannula. "Don't exert your memory. I'm Azerbaijani. Twice blighted since I don't belong to the Muslim majority. During the last days of the Russian rule we moved to Armenia but when war came we shared the fate of our fellow Azerbaijanis there. I guess I'm still counted among the million who remain homeless and internally displaced in Azerbaijan. Not that I should any more. Ever since I left the refugee camp and joined GAO, that has been my home."

Such a concise account. Such nonchalance. He'd thought her an enigma before, now…he just didn't know. Couldn't think. It was too much to take in. Impossible to imagine. Her life. A fifteen-year chunk of it. She must have been no more than thirteen or fourteen when it had all started. Had she lost her family? She'd said everyone she knew and loved. So she had. She'd been homeless and terrorized and abused, alone.

And there she was, surviving one war only to plunge, voluntarily, into another. Whatever her reasons for doing this, they had to be even more bizarre than his.

The fluid in both their bags had run through. She detached both lines, left the cannulae in and got up, avoiding his eyes. He watched her gathering instruments and supplies from his emergency bag and heading for the other casualties.

Dante felt the tug of oblivion, was tempted to just close his eyes and surrender to it. He couldn't. He'd saved one of the lives he'd been allowed. He still had another.

Gulnar. That was the only name that filled his awareness now, the only face he saw. Hundreds of people, all lives worth saving. But he had to choose one. He chose her. He had to.

A hand on his shoulder made him flinch. "It's me." He knew that. His body had thrilled to her touch. He'd know it anywhere now. She sank to her knees before him, exhaustion pinching her open face, hunching her strong shoulders. "I checked all the injured people and gave them antibiotics and tetanus boosters. Your blood seems to be of premium quality, too. They're reviving.

And they all thank you. One told me to tell you that no matter what happens to them from now on, in her book you've saved them.''

Dante's insides clenched. No, he hadn't. He wouldn't. In his book, all he'd done was torture them with false hope, prolong their suffering.

She cocked her head at him. ''What now?''

Dante's focus relinquished his internal agony for Gulnar's eyes. Could there be anything more beautiful? Was this why he'd decided on making her the lottery survival winner? Was he that basic?

No. She was more than a rarity of divine art. She was also a blinding manifestation of good. Few people had the capacity, the willingness to make a difference, to put themselves on the line for others. If he had to choose, it stood to reason he would choose the one most of use…

What was he thinking? How did he know that every other person here wasn't as useful in his or her own way? Who was he to decide who would do more good, who was more needed, more valuable?

It was more than cruel. Beyond monstrous. To be forced to choose. But he had to…

''Dr. Dante? Are you all right?'' Her solicitous stroke over his hand spread through him, the simple contact dousing him in unlikely, untimely sensations. Peace, pleasure. Arousal. It was just too funny to rediscover his libido now. But it wasn't why he wanted to save her. It wasn't!

He caught the hand covering his, stroked it back. ''I'm all right. Are you?''

Answering contentment softened her face, tightened her hand on his. ''I'm alive and conscious. So I'm all right.''

He nodded, groping for a way to disclose his grisly verdict.

He didn't have the chance. A probing expression invaded her eyes. "I told you what I am. You told me who you are, sort of, but you didn't tell me how you were allowed in here. The rebels have so far answered any approaches with a hail of gunfire and threats. It's why I thought you were with them in the beginning."

So she'd saved him the effort of stumbling through explanations, given him the shortcut to come clean after all. Answering her would still lead to confessing. "I have a…special deal with their leader."

Those eyes widened on astonishment and what else—suspicion? No. Just curiosity. "How so?"

So she didn't consider it even a possibility he was affiliated with the rebels! Good to know. "Two years ago, during an Azernian raid on his village, his wife and oldest child were almost fatally injured. I was roaming the area with another aid organization at the time and I happened to be in the right place in the right time. I saved their lives."

Gulnar gave a slow, thoughtful nod.

"Have you ever heard of Molokai?" Dante asked.

"Ah! It's almost common knowledge now that his group is the one that was responsible for Lorenzo's abduction, and the jet hospital's attempted hijacking."

That was something Dante hadn't known. More and more crimes, then. Dante gave the now seated militants a long look.

"When I heard about this attack and that he'd already announced he was responsible for it, I put a call out through his connections. He agreed to give me an interview, taking every precaution, of course. I demanded that he let me help the victims of this attack as I did his family."

"And he just granted your request?"

"I am here, am I not?"

"You mean he actually has a sense of fairness to appeal to? A sense of honor?"

"You'd be surprised how ruled by posturing and macho nonsense those people are. He made the mistake of having his right-hand man, the only one who speaks English among his men, present when he saw me, and I made sure the man knew what Molokai owed me. I think the fact that his men knew was the only thing that made Molokai agree to settle the debt, giving a speech about how he refused to be in debt to a foreigner who has no sympathy for his cause. He granted me two lives in return for his wife's and child's."

Gulnar's stare widened. Her words, when they came, were slow, realization tinging them with horror. "But you saved many more than two lives. At least twelve people would have eventually died without your intervention and your supplies."

She understood, but still needed him to spell it out. What the hell? He had to sooner or later. "They will all still die. He doesn't intend to let anyone, including his people, walk out of here alive."

He watched her eyes filling with terrible understanding. "And his people know that? That this is a suicide mission?"

"No, they don't. His plan is to stretch this out, get the most screaming tension out of the situation, the most international media coverage. Eventually his people will realize that the cavalry charge isn't coming—and that they will be left to die."

She interrupted. "And once they're desperate, it will get really ugly?"

"Probably. But this isn't the damage he's counting on. He mentioned something spectacular, alluded to how he *controls* the situation, and will *detonate* it when he deems it appropriate. I believe he has someone on the outside ready with a remote-control detonator."

Gulnar looked at their captors, cross-referencing his new information with what she'd gathered on her own. "They've been saying that the security forces outside can't help us—when the times comes we'll all be destroyed. At the time I thought they meant that they intend to go down for their cause, taking everyone with them."

"That's what Molokai intends to say when no one is left to talk. He intends to claim that his valiant warriors have laid their lives down for their cause. But I've learned from long service in chronic conflict areas that so-called suicide mission volunteers are invariably both conned and doped. Look at their eyes. They are addicts without even realizing it."

Gulnar's eyes followed his line of vision. "I've always wondered about that. And they have been smoking and snorting stuff."

"Drugs are spread throughout most rebel armies, touted as uppers and stamina boosters. The leaders enhance their men's malleability and subjugation with mental manipulation. Vengeful against a faceless enemy they've been bred to hate and coveting a higher status within their outfit are mixed with the inescapable chemical dependence to make the perfect mindless killing machine. They have no clue they're like thousands before them, just pawns who'll be used to spread chaos, then be disposed of."

He saw the certainty of doom sinking into her. None of the desperation, anger or horror were for herself. Her eyes didn't fix on him with an entreaty to choose her as one of the lucky two he'd save.

Not even momentarily to clamor for a chance to survive? Someone in the bloom of youth and beauty? How could she not have a shred of fear, an unreasoning desire to cling to life? It was inconceivable!

But maybe it wasn't. Maybe she had someone here

she would place far above her own life—without hesitation. A lover, perhaps.

His heart closed on a grating sensation. Disappointment? Bitterness? That Gulnar would die for another when Roxanne hadn't even been able to bear discomfort on his behalf?

But it wasn't bitterness. Roxanne, his family, everything and everyone in his past were long insubstantial, non-existent. None had a bearing on the present, on this moment. Gulnar filled those. A soul like he'd never encountered, one he had to preserve at any cost. He grasped her arm, urgency and a hundred other conflicting emotions boiling over inside him. "Gulnar, I want you to rise now, slowly, then we'll walk out of here together."

She pulled her arm back, slow, adamant. "I had a feeling you'd say that. Thank you, but, no, Dr. Dante. Save two of the injured."

He grabbed her arm again, pulled her towards him, kept her in place when she would have pulled back once more. "What makes them any more worthy of rescue than you?"

Her eyes squeezed shut. When she opened them again they were decided. Serene. "OK, so whomever you decide to save, the decision is skewed and the whole thing is just too macabre. But I don't want to be the one you rescue. I'd rather someone else survived this. I'll take my chances with the rest. If we're to die, as you said, maybe it's now my time."

"It isn't your time."

"How do you know that? It's not death but more abuse and torture that I'm afraid of. Save someone else."

He let go of her arm. He just had to press both hands to his head before it exploded with impotence and frustration and futility. "I want to save you all…"

"But you can't. And there's no telling when Molokai will detonate the explosives. So get out of here *now*, while you at least and two of your choice still can. This is a catastrophe and whatever you salvage out of it is better than nothing. Don't tempt fate any more."

So she understood how much he'd already tempted fate. Her insight was astonishing. The insight of someone who'd done her share of fate-tempting?

He had walked into the rebels' territory, expecting to be gunned down at any moment. When he'd reached Molokai in one piece, he'd just let him have his undiluted disparagement. He'd thought it would be the last thing he did.

Still, his gamble had paid off and it had gotten him here. And here he was, doing what he lived to do, giving people solace and reprieve, easing their pain and their degradation.

It was no longer enough. He couldn't do what he thought he had to. He, too, had thought two lives saved were better than none. But now he'd seen those people, now he'd tasted their desperation and resignation, now he'd touched Gulnar's life and power and selflessness, he knew he'd been wrong to settle for what he had, to bargain with the devil.

He wouldn't any more.

Decided, he sighed, drew Gulnar's swaying body into the curve of his. She flowed into him with no hesitation, burrowed deep. Hunger for access to her, for a connection, rose inside him like a tidal wave. He took her lips fiercely in brief, deep communion.

She didn't have a lover. He just knew it. She wouldn't fit into his flesh, merge with his fervor like this with an existing connection occupying her heart and tethering her senses. His heart lifted with the conviction.

How weird. To feel so upbeat at a time like this. When in a few minutes they'd probably all be dead.

CHAPTER FOUR

"ARE you ready to die, Gulnar?"

Gulnar's lips vibrated with Dante's words. Then her mind echoed with them.

Are you ready to die are you ready to die are you ready...?

She couldn't have heard right, could she? His words had mixed with their harsh breathing, her booming heartbeats. He couldn't have said that. Asked that.

But if he had, what did he mean? Was he saying goodbye? Or could he...?

Suspicion turned to conviction in a heartbeat. Terrible and insupportable, it cascaded through her, lurched her away from him. She had to read his intentions.

But she couldn't. She found herself gasping for their connection, for his breath. Horror, suspicion, the militants—nothing mattered. Resistance and caution were non-existent. She pressed back into the safest place she'd ever been. Him.

Yes. Whatever he meant. Yes. As long as he was here, she was ready to die.

Then he was no longer here, jerking away from her. Separation jolted through her, harder this time. A militant's heavy hand had landed on Dante's shoulder, pulling him away, ranting at him that he'd done what he'd come to do, to just wrap up and get out.

Gulnar's blood stopped in her veins at Dante's expression. *Just do what he says. Just get out.* It wouldn't take much now to drive the militant to defy his leader's orders, to negate Dante's special status. It would take far less than what Dante intended to do.

But maybe her suspicions were invalid. Maybe she'd superimposed her fears and a far-fetched meaning on his words.

His next words told her she hadn't. "Listen to me, Gulnar. I am this situation's last chance of resolution in something less than total loss. I have the best chance of doing something without being shot down on the spot. While their orders not to harm me still hold, I have to act."

God, *no*. He did mean to do something suicidal. Her cry for him to save himself was aborted by a harsher knowledge. His mind was made up. There was no changing it. Words scraped her on their way out. "What do you think you can do?"

"Anything is better than nothing."

"And two lives are better than nothing! Don't be crazy."

"I *was* crazy to even consider honoring that sadistic agreement. Two lives are *not* better than nothing, Gulnar. This way that monster makes me an accomplice in everyone else's deaths. It isn't happening. Everyone here gets an equal chance to survive. Or not. I can't— I *won't* choose." He cupped her cheek in his large palm, contained her agitation. She turned her face into it, her lips, drank deep of his conviction. "Will you help me, *bella mia*? I wouldn't have asked if you haven't already said you were unafraid, even willing to die. Now, if we do…"

She clung to his arms. He just had to listen to reason. He had to! "*We* don't have to do anything. *You* can walk out of here. *Please*, Dante…"

"No more Dr. Dante?"

"Oh, give me a break."

He pulled back, his black eyes devoid of intensity, obsidian wells of serenity, a tinge of almost-humor deepening their beauty. He continued as if she hadn't interrupted him. "*If* we do die, it will count for something, because we'd go out as fighters, not victims, and we'd probably end up saving far more than two lives. What do you say?"

So simple. So calm. As if he was asking her to take a ride with him, a ride with a very pleasant surprise at the end. What a man.

Oh, why hadn't she met him before? Why did she have to meet him now? Find out that he existed just a couple of hours before they had to die?

The possibility of violent, irrevocable loss had always been a fact of her life. She never got close, never let anyone close, expecting people to go away, to die or worse. Expecting herself to.

But she would have made an exception for Dante. She wouldn't have cared how soon he would have disappeared from her life. Or how. She would have taken her fill of him, fulfilled all fantasies, assuaged all hunger, if she'd only had a day with him. But she didn't have a day. Not even an hour.

She'd have nothing of him!

No! She'd already had. A lot. He'd given her so much. Much more than she had ever had. Solace. Strength. Wonder. Affirmation. And he would now give her the ultimate gift. He wouldn't leave her to die alone.

If she had to go, what better way to go than with him by her side?

She willed her lips to move in answering resolve and lightness. Anything seemed possible with him there, seemed worth it. Anything at all. And then some.

"So do we just charge them or do you have a plan?"

"I have a plan." He paused, his lips twisting. "Sort of."

"Reassuring!"

His lips spread in a smile. "It's still forming as we speak. Feel free to make amendments and suggestions. Here it is. We load all the Valium we have into syringes. Then I'll pretend that I have decided to leave. You will translate for me that I have chosen you and that guy over there to take with me."

Her heart picked up, sensing an emerging significance. "Anyan?"

"If that's his name. He's unable to move on his own and he's big enough that it'll take three men to carry him to the door for me."

It probably would. "What if they get suspicious? Ask why him specifically?"

He frowned. "You can say he means a lot to you—or something!"

Oh? "But will they believe me? I haven't come near him ever since I splinted his fractures."

His frown deepened. "You've been busy trying to tend to everyone's injuries. You are a nurse after all."

"I see. OK. And then?"

"You and I will hover around them, pretending to help, and while they struggle to lift him we will stick the Valium syringes into them."

Then it would all hit the fan. "And when they shout out, or decide to shoot us before they lose consciousness?" He had asked for amendments and suggestions, hadn't he?

He nodded, sighed. "I guess all we can do is make sure we inject the whole thing in one go. If we manage to hit a vein or an artery, they'd drop in a second.

Otherwise, we have to be ready with pads of cotton to stifle their shouts with.''

OK again. Maybe. A very shaky one. "What about the others? Where would they be while we're doing all that? Conveniently oblivious?''

He shrugged. "I am not saying this is iron-clad, but I am counting on the total boredom with me and what I'm doing that they've displayed so far. They haven't been watching us at all, and they have no reason to suddenly start watching us like hawks. I also bet they shove the hauling job onto their lowest ranking men. If they are who I think they are, we're in luck. These men are real slow.''

Well. "We come back to the moment we inject them. Even the slowest person in the world will yell in surprise and pain if stabbed with a three-inch needle. That's bound to get the others very interested in you!''

"Hmm.'' He rubbed his two-day beard, sexy and crazy and the most wonderful thing she'd ever seen. And nonchalantly planning their deaths. "How about we create a diversion, something loud enough to drown any shouts?''

Her body throbbed with his nearness. She forced herself to focus, raised her eyebrows. "How?''

"I have no idea.'' He actually grinned and she just wanted to devour that smile.

"I haven't thought that far. I thought if we got rid of three, and only five remained on this floor, it would encourage anyone who could get up to join us in charging the militants. I thought that if the militants shot us, the gunfire would make the security forces take a chance, bring them storming in from outside, changing the plan, rattling the outside agents, who would probably hesitate to act without their leader's order. My bet is until they inform him of the development and get his order to strike, it will buy enough time for the security forces to end up saving far more than two people.''

As plans went, this was one desperate piece of insanity. But as crazy as it sounded, it was the only thing that might end in less than total loss.

But wait—he'd said they needed a diversion, a loud one, and it had just occurred to her... If that idea could work, it would be just what they needed. And why shouldn't it? Still, she'd better run it by him, work out the bugs together.

He was already loading the Valium into their largest syringes. She joined him. ''I think I have an idea for that loud diversion we need.''

She rubbed her cheek over the nearest part of him, his shoulder. ''What I'll do is let the Azernians know that we need them to chant one of their patriotic songs. You know, pretend to be bidding us an emotional farewell. The hundreds of people around would be deafening at full blast. Now, even if they don't have enough lung-power they will probably make enough noise to drown out a couple of shouts. Even if they don't, the shouts may be interpreted as ones of outrage. This I can tell you, hearing the Azernian anthem will make the Badovnans real mad.''

The gleam in his eyes lit her up. ''Which will also keep their attention off us.'' His caressing pinch melted down her cheek to her lips. ''You're more than a genius, *bellezza*. This is an incredible idea. Do it. And be very clear when we need them to start chanting. We have to time it just right for it to work. The second Anyan is hauled up, they should burst into song. We probably won't have another chance.''

He moved to continue filling the syringes and she

stayed his hands. "What happens after we dispose of the first three?"

He pressed her to him for a precious moment. "If and when the others turn on us, we'll have their comrades' weapons in our hands and their comrades themselves in front of us as shields."

"You expect me to hold up an unconscious man?"

"I'll hold him up. You hide behind me."

Her eyes traveled down his formidable proportions. In normal conditions, she'd bet he could hold up all three he was bent on knocking out. Normal conditions these weren't. Another thing made her skeptical. "And you think it will give them pause? That they wouldn't shoot anyway, comrades or no?"

He handed her another Valium ampoule. "I hope it will make them at least hesitate. When they do, we explain their leader's betrayal, give them a chance to survive this. If they start shooting then, it's back to plan A and my hope that the forces outside come charging in."

"And what will we be doing in the meantime?"

"You find cover, you stay down, and you don't hesitate to shoot anyone who seems to be a threat to you or to others."

"And you?"

"I'll cover you."

"No, you won't. You'll do what you just told me to do."

"We may not need all this. We may get the militants to surrender."

"Yeah, sure. *Promise me*, Dante. No crazy heroics!"

He finished loading his syringes and raised warm eyes to hers. "I'll only do what needs to be done."

"That's not good en—"

His thumb on her lips didn't silence her. His eyes did. Eloquent. Decisive. Final. "Now, pretend to be doing a final check-up of the people you treated, pass your message around. Tell them to be careful not to arouse the militants' suspicion. Then come back to me."

The way he'd said that! Oh, God. It wasn't fair, not having more time with him. But she'd come back to him. They'd make their last stand together. It would be all that mattered.

He gave her hand one last bolstering squeeze and she swayed up to her feet, went to deliver her message, set the stage for the showdown.

The Azernians were wary, didn't want to antagonize their captors. She found no way around telling them what awaited them if they didn't co-operate.

Anyan was all for it. He hadn't been shot but beaten up. He had a fractured scapula and a shattered femur. Now loaded up on morphine, he felt invincible, and wanted to do whatever it took to take their oppressors down. She explained their plan to him, again and again. She didn't like the recklessness in his eyes.

Too late now to change their plans, to pick someone else. She left him and headed back to Dante. Dante. Even his name was magnificent. She wondered what it meant. And now she'd never know.

He had gathered all his stuff, closed the bag and was standing there, tall and indescribable, waiting for her to reach his side again. The militants by now considered her his, were no longer keeping an eye on her.

She smiled up at Dante, way up. It was the first time they'd stood up next to each other. He made her feel so petite. So feminine. So alive. Oh, Dante…

"All set?" She nodded and revealed the syringes stuffed into the waistband of her pants. His eyes rose from the sight of her naked midriff, tempestuous, locked with hers for an endless moment, everything exchanged and said. It could be the last glance. Probably was. ''Gulnar, whatever happens, it's been an honor.'' He took her hand, raised it to his lips, caressed each finger with a lingering kiss. ''You make me proud to be human.''

She couldn't hold back. She surged into him, encircled his body with both arms, ignoring the pain in her left one, the stiffness. Let the militants think it was gratitude for having chosen her for salvation. Or maybe as a bribe, a promise of favors to be bestowed if he chose her to save. Let them think whatever they wanted. They probably thought the worst by now. And it could only help their plan.

He pressed her head hard to his chest, over his booming heart. Steady, powerful. It was all there. His spirit, his virility, his humanity. She knew them all, down to the last detail. It had been three hours, and for ever, since she'd first laid eyes on him. She'd known what he was with that first look, against all damning evidence. It felt so good, made her so smug, knowing she'd been right about him.

Their embrace lasted for priceless seconds more, then they separated and he gestured towards the quarreling militants. ''Shall you do the honors?''

Without another look, she preceded him to the militants. He picked up his bag and fell into step with her. She stopped a few feet away from the militant pair, and explained Dante's wishes.

They called three of their underlings, the three Dante had predicted. They came lumbering over, sullen and sweaty, but it was clear they didn't even consider contesting their order.

They shuffled after Gulnar and Dante towards Anyan. Dante's gaze remained fixed ahead. They were getting what they needed, the militants' total disregard.

Their three helpers stood around considering Anyan's huge body and how to haul him from the floor without breaking their backs. Gulnar told them not to expect any help from him, warned them against causing him further damage, stressing their immediate and overall leaders' orders.

They fidgeted and gestured to Dante that they need a fourth for a safe lift. He pointed at his heavy bag. Giving up, they bent to the grinning Anyan. It took them half a dozen false starts to at last get a hold on him, their guns slung on their backs and their legs quivering beneath them under his unwieldy, flaccid weight.

The next second, every hair on Gulnar's body stood on end.

She'd been expecting it. But she couldn't have expected anything like this. The hostages' voices rose. But it wasn't singing, it was prayer. A requiem of defiance. Their voices rose, swelled, in impossible harmony, in soul-wrenching unison. The lyrics became holy, the melody magical. It was daunting, what they, with just their voices could do.

The Badovnan militants froze, spooked. Gulnar didn't wait for their paralysis to dissolve. Neither did Dante. They stabbed their targets with the tranquilizer. The militants' enraged cries were swallowed in the crashing waves of their hostages' passive aggression.

Dante barely caught Anyan before he crashed to the floor, dropped from limp arms. Then he and Gulnar snatched the rifles from the collapsing men. Dante managed to hold the biggest man up, hissed for her to stay behind him. It was all going according to plan.

Then it all went wrong.

One of the militants turned around, and he turned already firing.

No!

His gun spewed thunder and yellow bursts. Bright red exploded from the man in front of Dante, splattering her face, her left arm. He had just shot his colleague! There'd been no hesitation. No hesitation! And he kept firing. More crimson showered on her.

Dante!

Hearing the gunshots, the crowd hushed for a second then exploded on a sustained crescendo of desperation. Their effect was mind-bending. Their captors went berserk.

Then the rescue attempt started, the security forces blasting in. She saw Dante still standing, still holding up his murdered shield, firing back, saw the militant shake and convulse in a macabre dance, his body spewing blood.

"Dante! Get down!"

He couldn't hear her. Or wouldn't. Bent on protecting those flat on the floor, helpless. The security forces finished off the three militants at the door, turned on all the others who'd come rushing from their posts on the upper floors and roof.

Then an explosion brought half the ceiling hurtling down in boulder-sized chunks. The singing had stopped, a cacophony of panic and agony rising instead.

"Dante!"

She screamed his name. Wailed it. He didn't answer her. She couldn't see him any more. What if the security forces mistook him for a militant? What if he hadn't ducked out of the way of the debris in time? What if—what if…?

She scampered on hands and knees, frantic, crazed. And saw him. Dante! Standing and uninjured. Relief was brutal, enervating. Then it all went wrong again. The woman militant.

She'd circled behind them, was firing at him. *No.* No, she won't. Gulnar would shoot her first. And she did. Saw her stagger, red stains blossoming on her chest. Then she fell.

Dante turned to her, letting go of his bloodied shield. She erupted to her feet, flew towards him. He gestured with the gun, adamant, ordering her to stay there, stay down. Then his other hand went to his chest, came away drenched in blood. His eyes returned to hers again, stunned, questioning. His lips moved on her name. "Gulnar?"

Then he collapsed to the floor.

CHAPTER FIVE

"DON'T you dare die or I'll kill you myself!"

Gulnar. And she sounded incensed. Raw.

Dante opened his eyes and a scalding liquid splashed in his right one, forcing them closed again. But he'd already seen her incredible face hanging inches over his, ravaged, swollen. It was her tear that had fallen in his eye.

He tried to move, to reach out for her, protect her, soothe her. He couldn't. Searing lances in his chest pinned him to the floor. What was wrong with him?

Concentrate. Bring it back. Yes, there it was. The plan. The gamble. Gulnar right there beside him, unbelievable under duress, playing it all out with him. The Azernians joining in, overpowering in their desperation. Voices that could bring hell to its knees.

More memories rushed in. Stabbing their captors with the tranquilizer. One of the militants spoiling it all, killing his colleague without a thought. The man dying in his arms, his life seeping away with his consciousness, sensing the man's confusion, his anger, his terror.

The rest came crushing down. Firing the semi-automatic. The vicious intention to kill. Succeeding, killing one of the terrorists. So easily, over so quickly, the life spent saving others erased. The burst of savagery followed by unbearable nausea and horror. Then the security forces' unstoppable tide. The rest of the militants falling. Then the explosion and the building coming apart in monstrous chunks, crushing people. The screams. The screams!

But through it all, Gulnar's screams. It was those he remembered. Those that still shuddered through him. Her voice, rending on his name, bleeding black terror, tearing at him with the need to protect her—with foreboding.

Then an invisible lightning bolt tore clear through him, a blinding, viscous pain following, bursting, draining away whatever power he had left.

The woman had shot him in the back. It was over. At last.

But before he acknowledged the end, he turned to Gulnar, needing one last look, one last question. Was it really over? He'd never see her again?

And he let go. Died.

But if he had died, why was he a jumble of soreness and nausea and general misery? Was this what death felt like? It wouldn't be fair for death to feel so awful, so…corporeal. Shouldn't there be peace, reprieve—cessation? Of all physical sensations at least? Could this be the afterlife? When it felt too much like mortality? And what was Gulnar doing there? In his deathscape? Was he not yet dead? Was he still dying?

Oh, for God's sake, couldn't he just hurry up about it? What was he lingering for?

But he knew what for. Gulnar. She was all the reason he needed. To see her again. To at least say goodbye.

"You're not dying, do you hear me?"

And here was another reason. He didn't dare die, if it would anger her that much.

"Dante! Open your eyes, Dante! Now, damn you!"

Her yell tore through his quivering brain. Brought a smile bubbling from his depths. His lips couldn't comply. They were stiff and dry. Paralyzed. So were his vocal cords. But he had to try.

It sure hurt, producing sound through the sandpaper filling his larynx, sucking in air with the spears lodged all through his right side. Not to mention that air was screeching down his lungs from a suffocating vice clamped over his nose and mouth. Death by oxygen mask. Now, that would be novel.

"Promise me…you won't…rain tears in them again… first." His words came out rasped, smothered. He almost didn't understand them himself. "And…would you mind…letting me breathe…on my own?"

"Oh, Dante!" Seemed she understood him fine. Her trembling hands fumbled the mask off, then she hugged his head, his shoulders, racked him with her sobs.

His face burrowed in her hot, moist neck, his senses in her scent and anxiety and relief. She cared. Not about just another human being, but about him. And it no longer hurt. It was glorious. Could be addictive. He sighed and opened his eyes.

It was dark. And it wasn't him who had trouble seeing. The sun had long set. This meant it was more than a couple of hours since the crisis. Or was it another day altogether? His gaze panned around and it was only then that sounds registered, too. The frantic din of a huge accident scene.

So it was definitely the same day. He wouldn't avoid the immediate aftermath of the tragedy. He wasn't that lucky.

They were out in the open. The Azernian August evening weighed down on them with unforgiving humid heat. The building was in the background, hundreds of people dashing around, military, medical, civilians, and as many ex-hostages staggering zombie-like or strewn on the ground. He was one of the fallen, lying there prostrate, his upper body in Gulnar's lap. He stared up at her. A jeweled inky sky framed her now scarf-free, exquisite head.

Red. Deepest, richest vermillion. Her hair. It rioted out of an imperfect knot, waves of vital, vivid color. Even in the feeble streetlights, even after days of sweat and filth and abuse, it flamed, glorious, alive. He should have known it would be red. What other color could suit her? Express her?

Her tears splashed on his cheeks, his nose, trickled to his lips. He lapped at the precious drops. So good. Revitalizing. He sighed again. "I assume if I'm not dead, I've fainted. Again. This is getting embarrassing."

She didn't share his opinion. From the way her eyes blazed and her voice trembled she seemed to think it infuriating. "You idiot. You stupid, crazy fool! What did you think you were doing, when all hell broke loose and everyone was shooting at everything that moved, when everyone was flat on the floor and only you standing there, a seven-foot-tall target? What were you thinking, playing Rambo and all but screaming, 'Me, me, shoot me!'?"

He huffed a laugh. Huge mistake. It really hurt. "I'm...not seven-feet tall," he grunted. "That would make me...the Incredible...Hulk!"

"Don't you dare joke! Ooh, I'd hit you if you weren't already battered! You promised to get down, not to play any kamikaze tricks!"

"I said I'd do what needed to be done. In the heat of the moment, it seemed the only thing to do." More details bombarded him. People cowering on the floor, some still singing, until the few bullets had become a hail and their singing had fragmented, turning to cries of terror. There had been nothing to do but try to protect them. The scene around them now again tugged at his gaze. Something bitter spilled inside his chest. "And I'm not even sure I managed to do anything but kill everyone more quickly."

The touch of her freezing-in-cold-sweat hand jolted through him, warmed him to the core. He turned his face in her palm, his eyes going to her face.

Was that a smile? Yes. It was. Drenched in angry tears of relief and magnificent. "Believe it or not, you insane man, you didn't. Most of those people are just scared out of their wits, collapsed with dehydration and starvation. Only ten hostages died, and only twenty-three were seriously injured."

His breath hitched and the lances in his side and chest twisted. "Only?"

"Yes, only! Four hundred and forty-three are fine, will be back on their feet and leading normal lives in a couple of days, and it's thanks to you. I'd say that's a much better outcome than two. You were absolutely right. It turned out there were twenty-one more bombs planted and only one was detonated. They caught one of the men with a remote-control detonator before he had a chance to act. Seems the others ran away. The security forces still can't believe the way you've turned this around. They didn't even dream that when you walked in here, unintelligible and totally out of place, you'd turn out to be the wild card who'd turn that no-win situation around."

He had to wait until his heart unblocked his throat. "The wild card was you. I couldn't have done anything at all without you. I would have been dead and I would have gotten everyone killed. You saved my life. You saved those people."

She shook her head. "Oh, just take your dues. If you hadn't risked your life in the first place, thrown yourself into death's jaws, over and over, if you hadn't decided to either save us or die with us, I would have sat there and died with the others when Molokai decided to off us all for best effect."

"I'll take my dues if you take yours."

"Oh, all right. Let's agree to split the credit—and the blame."

So she was blaming herself for those who had died or been injured? For those they had killed?

A wave of tenderness swept him. His left arm was splinted to his side by her body. He tried to move his right one, to touch her, to soothe her, to feel that incredible, living mane for himself.

Wrong move. He doubted any move would be OK right now. His lung was scraping against his ribcage, muscles shredded, nerves exposed. "Tell me something," he gasped, making the pain even worse. "I am going to live?"

There was no mistaking the green flare in her eyes. He didn't need to see it to feel her concern, her anger at him for endangering himself, at the far worse fate he could have brought on himself. "You'd better!"

"I fail to see what I can…" He paused, waited out a spasm of searing pain. "Do about it if I don't. If I'm not mistaken, the woman militant shot me in the back and—"

She cut through his feeble words, reassuring, furious. "And the bullet went clear through you! It didn't hit the scapula, passed between your ribs, went through your right lung and out of your chest wall between the second and third ribs just beside the sternum. It hasn't touched any major vessels or structures and your lung has already re-inflated. You did lose blood before I collected some through the chest tube, but at least no more is coming!''

So that was what was lodged between his ribs! A chest tube—to evacuate the blood that must have accumulated around his lung. From the second, higher chest tube he could now feel, he analyzed the foci of agony. He'd bet he had a pneumothorax, too, with air leaking from his punctured lung and becoming trapped in the pleural space. No doubt the pressure of the accumulating blood and air had caused his lung to collapse. But the reason a tension hemo-pneumothorax was often rapidly fatal went beyond the blood loss or the collapsed lung. The rising pressure inside the chest caused displacement of the mediastinal structures and pressed on the other lung and the heart, interfering with, then stopping their functions.

The only way to stop the deterioration was to relieve the building pressure, inserting one chest tube in the chest to drain off the blood, and another high enough to let the accumulating air escape. And that was what she'd done—hadn't she? ''Did you perform the tube thoracotomies?''

Her snort was indignant. ''As if I'd let anyone else resuscitate you!''

This couldn't be good, the way his heart was ricocheting inside his chest. It couldn't be wise either, the way his deep-freeze was starting to thaw. The way he was starting to crave her caring. ''And by the feel of it, you didn't use local anesthesia before you shoved the tubes in my chest!''

Her touch melted, along with her luscious smile,

down his cheek, stroked him down to his soul. "We were fresh out of lidocaine. But I wasn't too concerned about the pain I would cause you. It was one more thing to stimulate you out of unconsciousness."

"Cruel woman." A couple of his fingers wrapped around a lock of hair, tugged. She came, willingly, gave him what would really revive him. Her taste, her breath. Her warmth and eagerness. She did all the work, moving her lips over his face, smoothing away the ordeal from his brow, taking the anger and horror and pain from his lips. He moaned it into her and she absorbed it all, imbued him with her vitality.

He felt his consciousness ebbing again. Felt like falling asleep. Hmm. What better thing than to fall asleep in her arms, with her lips on his face...?

Something wrenched him back, to suffer the pain and hear the weeping and scent the stench. Her loss. She was pulling away, leaving him alone and cold and bereft. His eyes snapped open to escape the nightmare, blurred over her image. Then his ears again rang with her frantic order. "Dante, stay with me!"

He winced, tried to pull her back, to dissolve in her warmth and nearness again. "Have mercy, Gulnar. I just want to sleep..."

She nudged him, gentle, then not-so-gentle, insistent, inescapable. "You're not going to sleep. You're going to sit up and drink. You've lost half of your blood between donation and injury. You'll enter irreversible shock if you don't replace the blood volume you've lost."

"Hook me to a fluid bag, *piccola*. I'll just take a little nap—"

"Don't *piccola* me! No napping, and we don't have

fluid bags to spare. Every one must be kept for the unconscious injured.''

He closed his eyes, nestled back into her firm, warm bosom. ''Consider me one of those…''

She pinched his arm, manually forced both lids open, peeling them off his unfocused eyes. ''You're not and you will not be again! You will drink and then I will take out the chest tubes, sew you up then take you for examination.''

''And then you'll take me home?'' Home. That was her place to him now. Where was that around here? Now, *that* was something to keep awake for, to be in it, with her—but he'd just rest for a while first…

No such luck. She nudged him again. ''C'mon. Open those eyes. Up, up!''

The woman was pitiless. ''Gulnar! I've been shot, for heaven's sake!''

''So? Nothing was really damaged. I examined you thoroughly while I was trying to find out where all the blood covering your right side was coming from.''

It was only then that he noticed. His blood-soaked shirt was closed over two large pads, one on the entry wound in his back and one over the exit wound in his chest, with slits through it for the chest tubes. Immaculate as usual. She must have taken his shirt off, examined him, performed the tube thoracotomies and put the shirt back on to preserve body heat. With his blood loss and shock he was still a prime candidate for hypothermia even in this heat. She'd done everything to the letter of the most advanced life-support protocols.

And to think she'd done it all, so thorough and efficient, minutes after surviving such horrors! What she must have felt, dealing with it all while coming to terms with having to kill another human being to save him, then still having him shot and possibly dying on her hands…

He needed to purge all her terror and helplessness, her stress and rage. But how, when he was the focus of her dissatisfaction? "You're angry with me, *bella mia*, aren't you?"

"Wow. What insight! Angry is too mild a word, Dr. Dante!"

"Oh, no! You've already called me Dante. You can't go back to calling me 'Doctor' now!"

"You don't want to know what I want to call you right now!"

"You mean beside idiot, insane and stupid?"

"Oh, that was the censored version of what I think of you for exposing yourself to needless danger, for—for…" Her voice choked, her tears flowed again. "I kept screaming for you to get down, to just get the hell down! It was as if you wanted to get yourself killed!"

Which could be an interpretation not too far from the truth. "Says the woman who refused a sure chance of survival!"

She wiped an angry hand across her eyes, adding another shade of smudging to her face. "I accepted death. I didn't invite it! Do you know just how lucky you've been?"

"Yeah. It's so weird. I thought I'd used up nine life-times' worth of luck in my life so far. Amazing to find out I still had some left over. I bet my luck has run dry now."

"It will if you don't shut up and drink!" She turned, grabbed a bottle up off the ground, put it to his lips.

He took an experimental sip. "Ugh. What's that?"

"A local drink."

"Tastes like the local refuse."

"Drink!"

"Tyrant." Her smile felt like a spotlight had been turned on, illuminating his heart. He gulped another mouthful. It tasted even worse. "Just thank God you don't have to drink this swill…"

She stroked his cheek, her smile widening. "I did drink it. Two bottlefuls."

"When you didn't need to? When no one was threatening to keep you awake until you did? Brave woman!"

The look she gave him! His heart swelled with pride and pleasure that she appreciated his lame jokes. "It's a potent folk remedy called Suakiri, made of an assortment of fermented seeds and molasses. High-calorie drink, packed with vitamins and minerals, all the things you need right now. The Azernians swear by it."

He mumbled something under his breath.

"What?"

He sighed. "Don't mind me. I'm just swearing *at* it."

Her bone-melting smile blossomed into a giggle. She resumed stroking his cheek and watched him as he gulped the first few swallows. It felt as if he'd forgotten how to drink. He had no co-ordination. Whether due to her touch, or with depletion, he had no idea.

It wasn't until the liquid started running down his chin that her face pinched on a surge of renewed worry. She adjusted his head and the bottle. "Easy. We don't want you to choke. Not a good idea to cough now."

"As if I even could. If any liquid goes down the wrong way, you'll have to aspirate my trachea."

"Dante, shut up and sip."

He did. Surrendered to her ministrations, sipped and moaned his enjoyment at her stroking. He even thought he purred. It was amazing. There he was, in the aftermath of a traumatic situation, feeling so good, so contented. It had to be shock.

And that Suakiri must really have magical powers. Life was seeping back into him with every sip. Must get the recipe. But he still wanted to sleep. Not the fading away of depletion, but the repose of recharging. He took the last gulp, hummed his satisfaction, adjusted his position and closed his eyes.

"Time to recheck you!" Gulnar substituted her lap for a folded towel below his head and undertook his reassessment with dogged determination.

"Gulnar, I'm fine. You've saved me. Again."

"Let me be the judge of that!" She opened his shirt, slipped his arm out of one sleeve and recorded his pressure.

"One-ten over seventy, right?" Her astonished glance rested on him for half a second then she removed his pads. "I can tell. And I can tell you, whatever danger I was in, I'm past it. If you have other patients to see to, you can go now. I'll just rest until you come back."

"There are dozens of medical personnel on the scene now, more than enough to handle all the injured. And until it is your turn to ride in one of the ambulances going to and from Srajna General Hospital, you're not sleeping, and that's final." He opened his mouth. Her hand below his chin closed it for him. "Can you sit up?"

He scowled at her and did, feeling the assortment of spears embedded in him shifting, introducing him to new levels of pain. "It's a bunch of rubbish, you know, this myth about a trauma victim deteriorating if you let them sleep."

"I know. I'm just being unscientifically paranoid. Humor me."

He watched her eyes misting in the dimness as she rechecked both the entry and exit wounds, made sure that the blood level in the underwater-seal bottle was no longer rising now he was sitting up and in a position for better drainage. She seemed to be debating whether to leave them in or take them out. She shared her diagnosis with him, sought his. "I think there will be no more bleeding, that I can remove the chest tubes. What do you think?"

He looked down his chest, and only saw her splayed hand over his tensing muscles just below the wound. Images of catching that hand in his teeth and sucking each of her fingers completely into his mouth mushroomed. He winced, prayed that darkness was obscuring his blatant, idiotic reaction.

"What's wrong? Oh, lie down again!"

He didn't know whether to be thankful or exasperated that she had misinterpreted his state. "It's nothing I can't handle." Which was an outright lie. *Focus, Guerriero!* "And I think your diagnosis is correct. This looks self-limiting. I think you can remove the upper chest tube. And I bet most of the bleeding wasn't from the lung injury, but from a couple of torn intercostal and mammary arteries. Bet they went into spasm, made a healthy clot. As long as my pressure holds, I don't think there's any problem. But to be on the safe side and save you from introducing another chest tube if I start bleeding again, just fold the lower one in place and apply a bandage over it. If in a few hours there's no more bleeding, you can remove it."

Her nod accompanied a sigh of relief and a tremulous

smile. She extracted the chest tube so gently he didn't feel it being pulled from deep within his chest.

He drew a deeper breath, felt a rush of air and life and gratitude. He'd walked into the rebels' stronghold yesterday, then into that municipal building today, with the willingness to end it all hovering at the periphery of his mind. But now he was fiercely glad that that woman hadn't succeeded in killing him. Gulnar inhabited this world and he wasn't in any hurry to leave it now.

Humor her? He'd do anything at all for her.

CHAPTER SIX

"WILL you do something for me?"

Gulnar met Dante's eyes in the mirror, watched his left hand rubbing his three-day beard. He should look like hell. He did—yet was still heart-stopping.

His eyes flickered in uneasy entreaty, his voice dipped to danger level. "Please?"

Her bones increased their melting rate. Soon he'd have to scoop her off the floor.

Did he really think he needed to be uncomfortable asking her anything? Didn't he know she needed no amount of persuasion, would have no hesitation to do anything for him, to let him have anything at all? Just as everyone else would be falling over themselves to give him the moon, and any other planet that he might fancy?

He should know. But he didn't, even after being shown, in every way. It said a lot about him that he still didn't accept everyone's esteem and appreciation, didn't acknowledge that he deserved them. He acted as if he'd done nothing at all. She'd never seen anyone more uncomfortable with attention and gratitude.

Ever since officials and reporters had milked the distraught survivors for every last bit of detail about the crisis, Dante had been fighting off both.

It hadn't been easy, calming the over-zealous reports, with her in the middle translating both ways, trying her best to prevent the crisis from metamorphosing into a myth.

But there had been no stemming the tide of the excited masses that had swooped down on them, proclaiming him a national hero. He had been all but wrapped in cotton wool and swept to Srajna General Hospital, with every high official and security chief trailing ahead and behind their ambulance in a stately motorcade. They had even followed them through ER then every diagnostic suite as a dozen emergency doctors, radiologists and trauma surgeons had hovered over Dante, performing all kinds of unnecessary tests and taking every far-fetched precaution.

She had continued translating Dante's insistence that she'd already done all that needed to be done, that all that remained was a simple chest X-ray to see if there wasn't a residual clot around his lung, that all other costly tests were unnecessary. His insistence that as a trauma surgeon himself he should be allowed an opinion of his own condition had been overridden. Then his objections had grown stronger, and her translations more selective.

When all else had failed, he had demanded, loudly, to be left alone.

That needed no translation.

And that was when her role was considered over and she was herded out with the departing people. Frantic to be torn away from Dante's side, she almost burst into tears of gratitude and relief when he clung to her. But to her distress he didn't stop there. He forced her to translate to the crowd his indignation at their dismissal of her role in it all. "Just tell them what I'm saying," he persisted. "Word for word, Gulnar. I'll know if you're watering it down."

She needn't have worried about his extravagant report, though. No one was inclined to believe that she was the real hero, the one who had snatched him from death's jaws twice, and the reason all those who'd survived had. It was more palatable for them to believe a man of Dante's stature and abilities to be the real and sole hero of the day.

Though she was happy to fade into the background, to get no recognition or gratitude, their prejudice still rankled. Chauvinist pigs!

But, to be fair, women thought the same. Even more. Chauvinist race, it seemed.

To further clarify her status in his eyes, he ordered a bed to be brought in for her in his room, made it clear she was the one to consult with about his condition, that she would be his companion until he was out of the hospital. Then he growled them all out of their room.

After freshening up all he could, he sat there in bed, envying her her no-holds-barred shower, huge and haggard and just too much for her battered senses. Then he asked her permission to sleep.

Torn between wanting to howl with laughter at his small-boy-asking-mama's-consent act and her phobia of seeing his eyes closing, she forced herself under control. The man had to sleep some time. To save her sanity, she planned to stay awake beside him, counting his breaths. That sanity evaporated when he raised exhausted eyes to her and asked for a kiss goodnight.

It was as if a dam had burst. Tenderness swelled and crashed inside her. She wanted to throw herself at him, but couldn't, dammit. He could barely breathe without moaning in agony, analgesics and all. But when she took his lips, he sank into instant slumber, his groan becoming one of contentment, reverberating on her lips, in her soul. She cast a look at her bed then curled herself in the few inches of space beside him.

She began her vigil, lost count of the times she counted his heartbeats, soothed his starts and sent up prayers of thankfulness for his survival, for his very existence, and a plea for his recovery.

It was so weird. She was beyond finished. Beyond devastated. The ghastly memory of taking another's life, no matter how justified, and the nightmares of every complication he could suffer were tearing at her. Yet she wasn't wishing all those horrors erased, like she did those before them. They had introduced her to him, and he was part of them and she would cling to their memory, scars and nightmares and all.

She eventually succumbed to her own fatigue, but only when his vital signs remained steady and strong. She woke up to his body fused to hers, to his gaze tender and restored. It was such a privilege, such luxury to lie there, staring at him, exchanging expressions of gratitude for sharing the ordeal, halving the burden of recollections.

Then he advised her to get out of bed. He was hungry enough to eat her. She would have offered herself as fast food if she hadn't needed to take care of him first.

The morning nurses came in and tried to do that. He wouldn't let them. He wanted no one else near him. Gratitude, relief and pride choked her as she fed him breakfast and tended to his medical needs.

Not that anyone but him trusted her measures. With the morning rounds, the hordes of doctors were back, checking and double-checking them. Dante conceded that the fastest way to get rid of them was to go with the flow. This time he let them satisfy themselves, ooh and aah over his luck and improvement. Once the test results were back to confirm his stable condition, the happy news was announced to the panting press and representatives of the Azernian town whose people had been involved in the hostage situation. Then they were let in to visit him.

They got Gulnar's rushed thanks out of the way before turning the full force of their gratitude on Dante. She tried to convey Dante's discomfort at the extravagance of their emotions, but it only raised him higher in their eyes. They kept asking what they could do for him in return. It was clear that at the height of their emotions these people would have laid all their belongings, all their daughters at his feet.

No, scratch that. The daughters, and every other woman of every age and marital status, would hurl themselves there. No question.

He was turning away from the mirror now, bringing back that first moment when she'd seen him walking into that hall. After all he'd been through, poetry still coursed in his every move. Looking imposing and majestic in the ridiculous just-below-the-knee hospital gown had to be some world precedent, too!

She waited for her breath to return, her heart to resume beating. No such luck.

What was the matter with her? She'd already shared with him the most traumatic experiences two people could share, had had her hands all over him in every possible way—well, not every one, but she had kissed and fondled him. She'd slept with him—OK, beside him. But to be shy now? When she'd never known what shyness was? For heaven's sake!

Her mind was incredulous but her body was going to pieces, her heart staggering in her chest with his every step closer.

Look away. Make a joke. Do something.

She escaped his intense gaze, only to find hers rushing down his body, greedy, feeding her rioting thoughts, inflaming her simmering senses.

She had noted the chiseled perfection of his torso and back while treating him. But it had been out of the question to salivate over them then. Now, with her body rested and replenished, with him out of danger, it was a different story. It was beyond her to resist making a visual feast of the rest of him, especially the parts she could see clearly, his legs, oh, my—those legs! She saw them between hers…

He stopped just a foot away. Oh, hell, he had to see her condition, read her thoughts. His gaze was burning. Then he dropped it.

He looked away, exhaled. "You won't have to do anything else for me again, promise." He paused, a grimace of disgust twisting his expressive features.

He really didn't like imposing on others in any way, didn't he? He really thought it was less than a total pleasure, tending to his every need. Time to disabuse him. "Let's get one thing straight here, Dante. You can ask anything of me."

Obsidian eyes turned on her now, explicit, stormy. "*Anything*, Gulnar?"

Oh, yes. *Yes!* Anything at all.

Reason tried to intrude, to point out their situation, his shooting just fourteen hours ago. Reason didn't have a prayer. What was it anyway? Just stupidities and shackles designed to waste life and chances and foster regrets and bitterness. If he wanted her, if he would have her, she'd offer herself. She did, made the offer open-ended, total, unconditional. "*Anything*, Dante."

He bent slowly, holding her eyes until he took her lips in a fierce press. In only seconds he stepped back, still uncertain. She pulled him back, her wary self-consciousness gone, the unconditional tenderness she reserved for impersonal duty, the unguarded faith opening her arms around him and her mouth to his tongue.

"Dante…" His name sighed on her lips, a celebration, a supplication, a second chance at life. Her first real chance. He absorbed it into him, took her lips, her breath, like their first kiss. And nothing like it. No tender reassurance here. There were no preliminaries, just all-out invasion and headlong surrender. Never before. This connection, this pure craving, this clear access to another. She had never even imagined this mix of lust and trust, carnality and vulnerability.

She'd been waiting for this for ever. For this man. And she'd never even known. Never known there was that much to dream of. Had it really been only a day? Yes, and it had been her real lifetime, erasing her barren existence before it. It was enough to know he existed, that she could feel this way. She'd never ask for more. Never be the same.

He staggered back, sagged down on the couch, keeping their lips fused, tried to bring her down on his lap.

She resisted his hungry power. "I'll hurt you…"

His groan reverberated inside her. "I hurt more where I'm not touching you. Touch me, Gulnar, give me your mouth, your body."

His need sent hers raging, sank her into his mouth again, gasping for him. His breath filled her lungs. Just hours ago, he'd had none. He'd nearly drowned in his own blood, suffocated on his own breath. The tears that had poured out of her soul as she'd struggled to restore his ability to breathe welled again, flooded both their faces. He licked them all, murmured his craving, his soothing, nipped her quivering chin, stilled it in his teeth.

"Dante, you're in pain—every time you draw breath…"

His grunt confirmed her words, the sound so deep and dark it scared her, aroused her beyond endurance. He only pulled her back into his kiss, muttered against her lips, "Then you kiss me, Gulnar—save me the effort. Let me feel you, *tesoro*, feel your heat and life and desire."

She could resist her hunger, for his sake. No way could she withstand his. She capitulated, straddled his thighs, hers taking her weight, her arms keeping her torso off his. He wouldn't let her keep that distance, his left arm pressing her down and forward.

"Dante!" It was too much—too poignant, feeling him hard with life and arousal. The promise of all that power inside her, the completion, the merging. He snatched his lips from hers to bury his pained pleasure in her neck. She rained her own kisses all over the slashed planes of his face, scraping her abandon across his beard.

"Help me…" His left hand wasn't up to opening her shirt unaided. She was up to doing anything he wanted and what he wanted was more of her flesh, her willingness. She'd give him all.

Another surge of moist heat flooded her, demanding him inside her, granting them both release and oblivion. Her lips fed at his pulse as she fell into his rhythm, their clothes a chafing barrier. She unbuttoned her top, and what he did then stopped her heart.

He just laid his face against her breasts and breathed her in, breathed out her name almost like a mantra, a prayer. For endless minutes they just stayed there, with his head hugged to her breast, her heart beating just because he'd said her name.

Then he rubbed his face over her breasts, had her writhing before his lips closed over one nipple. She arched on a seizure, on a mute scream. She knew her body, her senses. They weren't equipped to register that much. Never had there been sensations fiercer than caution, greater than detachment. It had to be him, his effect, causing her metamorphosis.

His eyes captured hers, showing her what it would be like with him driving inside her, filling, inflaming, assuaging. Her muteness shattered, her cries rose, her disbelief, too. Just promising her with his eyes and he was bringing her closer to an unknown cataclysm. Her tremors became quakes.

"Gulnar—from the moment I first saw you, do you know what I wanted to do to you? With you? For you?"

His words, the total abandon they painted, every license she couldn't wait to grant him. They released her from the crippling build-up, completing the climax that drained her, left her hungrier. The hands that held his head to her breast tore at his headscarf, needing her fingers in his hair, luxuriating and—she froze.

No hair. He had no hair!

Surprise flooded her, immobilized her. Then curiosity swelled by degrees. Dante, without the presumed dark wavy hair? She finally jerked away, bracing herself for a different Dante from the one already imprinted on her awareness, and—Oh!

Her every mental image and presumption disintegrated. What were those compared to his reality?

He—he looked as if he'd just stepped out of a medieval fairy-tale! A knight sworn to an ascetic order—shaved and fasting, perpetually prepared for to-the-death battles!

And he wasn't shaving the rest of balding hair, like

so many men did. A barely there raven shadow clearly delineated his healthy hairline. But it would have been a crime to cover such perfection with hair, no matter how luxurious. He just had to know how unique a shaved head made him look. If he didn't, her stunned hunger would surely tell him.

"Oh, Dante…" Her eyes closed as she reached for him, her hands itching to experience his regal symmetry and strength in unhindered touching.

He aborted her eager grope, pushed her hands away. She almost stumbled off his lap. Her heart did, plummeted all the way down to her gut.

He was withdrawing, all intimacy leaving his expression, distress, disappointment flooding in its wake.

She sat still, sick electricity arcing in her flesh, waiting for him to spell it out. He did, and life dimmed back to its dreary monotone.

"Hell, I'm sorry Gulnar…" His strident breath wheezing out of him, he slumped back, closed his eyes. Then he opened them, turbid and disturbed and averted from her still-exposed breasts. "You're suffering from post-traumatic stress and I took advantage of it…"

His agitation hurt her even more than his withdrawal. She had to relieve it. Had to cover herself first, get off him. Had to find her co-ordination and control. She finally did, stumbled up and to her bed, sank on it, aftershocks of release still rocking her, loss and confusion suffocating her.

He continued, his black-velvet voice hushed. "I can only plead that I must be suffering the same survival backlash…"

"You said you felt this way from the moment you saw me…" Please, let this at least be real.

His next words told her it wasn't. "I guess, being in

this region, in our line of work, we're never not in post-traumatic stress. What we think, and what we think we feel, how we react—it's all extreme reactions, unreal, just escape mechanisms."

She was intimate with all that. The last fifteen years had been a string of coping maneuvers, sanity preservers. She'd mastered them all. And none of them applied here. With Dante, it was all new and real at last.

And it was one-sided.

Fine. She understood. It gutted her, but she did. And she accepted it. She would still have something else of him. He was part of GAO now. They were bound to give him an important post, keep him here. She'd join his team. It would be enough to see him, work with him. Anything at all with him was better than everything she'd ever had…

He finally moved, rose, came over to stand above her, every move an effort now. "Gulnar, please, say you forgive me. I feel like I've dishonored what we've shared, what we've been through. And after all you've done for me. I can't let us part with this hanging between us."

Part? Did he think he needed to put distance between them now? Would he ask for an assignment that would take him out of her reach? Refuse her access to his team?

No. No! She had to make him understand it wouldn't change a thing, that she wouldn't pursue or embarrass him. Their enforced intimacy was over and she'd keep to her place, be his assistant, or whatever he wanted her to be, and nothing more. She had to make him believe her.

"Dante—stop it, please. You're making too much out of this. It isn't the first time and it won't be the last that two survivors seek physical comfort in each other's arms.'' A bitter giggle escaped her. She surely hadn't given him comfort! ''I can't begin to see how you can think you've dishonored anything.''

The distress in his eyes faded, something even blacker, bleaker seeping into its place. Then his lids went down, obscuring a succession of expressions that stopped her heart. Cynicism. Disillusion. Disgust.

He walked back to the couch, sat down again. His head fell back on the headrest, his lips twisting. Her insides followed suit. Had she made things worse by making light of it? Was he, now that his blood had cooled, analyzing her actions, condemning her for her shamelessness, seeing her as Lorenzo—and Emilio—had once accused her of being, a promiscuous hazard to any team effort? No!

She tried again, an uncontrolled thread of desperate laughter weaving into her tones. ''Dante—let it go. It was nothing important, really. A month from now we'll look back on this and laugh.'' Stop, stop. She was making it worse and worse. Distract him. Change the subject. ''And do you realize you didn't tell me what you wanted me to do for you? Do you need your back scratched?''

The eyes that opened, leveled on her, were a stranger's.

So this was how it felt to lose something irreplaceable.

''Actually, I was going to ask you to shave me, especially my head. I don't mind the beard as much, but a few millimeters' growth on top makes me crazy.'' Even his voice was unrecognizable.

Swallowing the jagged desperation, she jumped at the opportunity, and to her feet.

His alien voice froze her. "Never mind. I don't think you're in any condition to handle a razor now. What you really need is to get back to sleep. I'll take one of the other nurses up on her offer."

Other nurses? Oh.

That put her in her place. Ended their artificial intimacy and her importance to him.

But this was what she'd said she'd settle for! Keep it light. Impersonal. He wanted it that way.

Her heart wept but she tried on her most nonchalant smile. "Just to put your mind at ease, I'll let someone else do it. But for future reference, I'll have you know that I am an expert barber!"

His blank eyes rested on her, his smile even emptier. "I'm sure you are. But since I'm going back to the US just as soon as I can breathe without keeling over, I don't think I'll have the chance to take you up on your offer."

CHAPTER SEVEN

"You just can't leave!"

Dante sighed. GAO's Azernian operation coordinator was a good man. One of the best. He just had the most aggravating nasal twang ever. As for his powers of repetition!

Dante inhaled deeper this time, the air rushing into his lungs a reminder of how lucky he'd been. Only two weeks after a bullet had penetrated his chest back to front, he was beyond lucky to be breathing at all, let alone with such ease.

No, it wasn't luck. It was Gulnar…

"Dr. Guerriero, you have to let us persuade you to stay longer!"

Impatience chafed in Dante's chest, the currents stronger along the fast-healing bullet tract. "Mr. Kauffman, you have to stop talking as if I'm going back on my word, as if I'm deserting! You knew the moment I stepped into your office two weeks ago that I was here for the hostage situation, not to join GAO. I am sure you also know that I am a freelancer, if the term can apply to voluntary work. I roam around offering my services where I can make a difference, then move on. I couldn't have been clearer when I asked you to grant me temporary GAO credentials. As it turned out, it has been the only thing that has gotten me through the quarantine zone. Now it's over, and so is our liaison, and I'm moving on, as has always been my intention."

Kauffman's lanky, relaxed posture eased even more,

making his persistence even more droning, more effective. "That's all well and good, as far as previous plans go, Dr. Guerriero. But things change. Things have changed."

Dante stared at the fair, frail man who'd had him trapped in this office for the last hour. Who had him trapped, period. Dammit. What a disguise! Ivan Kauffman was anything but fragile. He'd never come up against fiercer relentlessness. He'd dragged him into a logic loop, and every time they bounced the same argument off each other, Dante felt his grip on his slipping. Ivan made him feel like trash for doing what he'd been doing for the last four years, something he'd thought effective and worthwhile.

He shook his head. The man was a juggernaut. He should have known he would be one. People who picked humanitarian work in the most dangerous places on earth were a special breed. They had to have steel running through them, had to be totally unpredictable. Like Gulnar...

"We don't only need any and every capable medical person around here." Kauffman made his main argument again, tireless, tiring to his listener. "But after what you've done, you're not just an extra pair of sorely needed hands. Like it or not, you are a role model, a symbol of hope that good does triumph over evil and that humanitarian operatives are not just more vulnerable chips for terrorists to play with."

Counter-arguments crowded into Dante's mind. None of them seemed enough any more. He exhaled, irritated, cornered and hating it. "Really, Mr. Kauffman! This legend everyone is weaving around my role in the hostage situation is getting out of hand."

"Modesty is very becoming, Dr. Guerriero, and also

the mark of a true hero.'' Oh, no. He didn't get him that way. Dante had no ego to tickle in this direction. Kauffman continued, exchanging flattery for debate, ''How many doctors breach impending disaster situations and not only manage to save almost everyone, but come out alive, too? Even we who live and work in areas of conflict do so only where there is relative safety. We take precautions and withdraw from openly dangerous situations. Not many risk throwing themselves into the line of fire, and almost none who actually do make it out get their charges out, too. This has been epic, and you'd better get used to it.''

Dante's teeth screeched against each other. What he'd give for an episode of mass amnesia to counteract the sweeping mass hysteria! When would it pass? He just wanted to fade into the background, wipe this from the record, get on with his roaming—get away from Gulnar…

He exhaled again. ''You know what, Mr. Kauffman? I was really indignant when you all insisted on downplaying Gulnar's far more important role in this situation. Now I am just glad everyone decided to ignore her. I have never suffered anything more aggravating and oppressive than the status you've all thrust on me. I am happy she escaped the same fate.''

Kauffman gifted him with another of those impassive smiles that made him feel like an over-emotional idiot. Made the man such a nerve-fraying negotiator. ''Such is the burden of heroism, Dr. Guerriero. Just as you'd accepted the possible outcome of severe injury or death, going in there, you have to accept the acclaim now you've made it out triumphant. And you also have to accept the responsibility that acclaim places on you.''

Dante heaved himself up to his feet. This wasn't going to end unassisted. "That's where you're wrong, Mr. Kauffman. I don't have to accept anything. In my opinion, I've done my share, and that's it. I'm out of here, and I'll be eternally in your debt if you stop your attempts to emotionally blackmail me into staying, and if you let this be the end of this endless meeting."

Without giving Kauffman the chance to bat a languid eyelid, Dante dragged the man's hand for a hard, adamant handshake then turned and almost ran out of his office. And directly into Gulnar. And Emilio.

His heart stuttered. Everything inside him surged, almost burst out of him. *Why didn't you come to see me today?*

He barely caught the reproachful roar back. She didn't owe him anything after that morning when he'd behaved like an out-of-control teenager. She'd been gracious enough to laugh it all off and walk out of his room with a smile.

The moment she'd closed the door behind her he'd plunged into a hell he'd never known before. Not knowing if she'd ever return, where she was, how to contact her, what he'd say if he did—he'd felt abandoned, desperate, like a kid in an alien world, and it had had nothing to do with her loss as an interpreter.

Next morning, and every day ever since, she'd come back during the morning visiting hour, ten to eleven a.m., behaving as if they hadn't fought and survived by each other's sides, as if they'd shared nothing but an aborted flirtation in one of his former American hospital's cafeterias. And she'd mostly come with her shadow, her fellow GAO volunteer and nurse, the hunky Emilio Fernandez.

He'd lived for that hour. Then she'd deprived him of it today. The almost suicidal despair that had robbed him of all reason and power when the seconds had ticked by and she hadn't appeared had decided him. He was running out of there.

Tomorrow. He'd go back on the road tomorrow. And to hell with recuperation.

"Dr. Guerriero! Good thing we caught you. We were told this was one of your stops today." It was the Portuguese nurse who addressed him. Gulnar only looked at him. Burned him down to the bone.

He swallowed the roiling hunger, the crushing despondency, kept his eyes on Emilio. "Yeah, I have a whole line-up of appointments all over Srajna."

Emilio raised one thick, straight eyebrow. "People actually asked you to go to them?"

Say something cool and diplomatic. "I'm a popular man nowadays, am I not, Fernandez? Everyone wants a piece of me." OK, not so cool or diplomatic. "Most did try to save me the trouble, but twelve days in one place, one room, is my limit. So, what can I do for you? I really have to run."

Emilio's brown eyes told him he could drop dead. At six feet five it was unusual for Dante to meet men's eyes on the same level. He did Emilio's. A mane of black curls even gave the good-looking man an extra inch over him. As tall and as broad and as dark. Emilio could have been his brother. And he hated Dante's guts.

It figured. Men who were interested in Gulnar would probably shred each other with bare teeth and talons over her. And Emilio's interest was unmistakable. Was Dante's?

What kind of a stupid question was that? All the sexual energy he'd thought he'd never had or had lost had only been accumulating undiscovered, had only taken the sight of her, her touch to be unearthed, unleashed.

But once he was out of her orbit, he'd revert to his usual numbness. He'd throw himself into the sanctuary of emotional vacuum again. He couldn't wait.

Emilio's lips stretched on a pseudo-smile, revealing white, clenched teeth. Only fair. Emilio set Dante's teeth on edge, too. "Nothing you can do for me, that's for sure."

A subtle communication passed between Gulnar and Emilio. Reproach on her side, he-had-it-coming sullen protest on his. Dante felt more lost and alone watching their unspoken argument, the ache of alienation spreading, worse than all his years of estrangement put together. That was an exchange born of entrenched familiarity. And intimacy?

Jealousy seared through him. How stupid was that? How pointless when he wasn't entitled to it? But stupid or pointless or not, he barely stopped himself from putting his fist into Emilio's challenging face.

As if he could. His right arm was functioning again, but there'd be no punch-throwing. Never had been and never would be. Not if he wanted to remain a surgeon. But he'd been certain she wasn't involved. Had he not sensed her involvement with Emilio because he didn't want to? Or because it didn't count to her? Just as their encounter didn't?

Was this how it always was with her? All attachment was on the side of the stupid, addicted males?

And Emilio was certainly attached—not just attracted, but emotionally attached. Yet even in his presence Dante still didn't pick an answering attachment from Gulnar. That didn't mean there was no involvement. It could be a purely physical, unemotional interest on Gulnar's side.

Gulnar and Emilio had fallen into brisk step with him

as he hurried out of the small building housing GAO's modest rented administration office.

He added to his speed. He didn't want to be in their company, didn't want to know what went on between them. If they hadn't come after him now, he would have left tomorrow first thing in the morning before Gulnar came on her daily visit, if she came. He wouldn't have seen her again, he would have run without saying good-bye...

He flicked Emilio an impatient glance. "So what's the emergency? I hope it's something simple for a change. I don't have time to deal with anything more. I'm leaving tomorrow."

"You are?" Gulnar spoke for the first time, her velvet voice scraping his exposed nerves. "But you're not fully recovered yet!"

They'd reached his ride, the stately diplomatic limousine the Azernian president had put at his disposal. His uniformed chauffeur was leaning on the hood, smoking. He straightened as soon as he saw him, jumped forward to open his door for him. Dante shook his head at him, his lips going numb. An escape car and no way to escape! Not until he got rid of Gulnar and Emilio. "I'm fine. My luck is holding out. The bullet couldn't have picked a lesser damage route if it had meant to, and my blood picture is almost back to normal, so I'm almost as good as new."

"But you should be in hospital for another week," Gulnar insisted. "Then you should recuperate for another two! All doctors said so!"

"So we're back to ignoring the fact that I'm one myself, eh?" She opened her mouth. He just couldn't bear hearing her voice again. He raised his voice, drowning hers. "My professional opinion says I'm well enough to leave tomorrow, and I will. Anyway, if people keep demanding things from me, they must think me well enough. So what am I needed for now?''

He could have sounded less fed-up, should be accessing his professionalism. His despondency wasn't Gulnar's or Emilio's fault. Or anyone's. Or life's.

Emilio slowed down, stopped, his hostility even more evident. ''We're so sorry to impose on the time and plans of the madly-in-demand, exalted hero of the Caucasus. But your even more exalted talents as a reconstructive surgeon are being called upon. If you deem it worth your while, of course.''

OK. That was deserved. But it wasn't in answer to his unintentional arrogance. This was personal. And beyond the instinctive antagonism between two males over a coveted female. Why? Had Gulnar told him what had happened between them?

But what had happened? Nothing much, she'd made it clear. Just the inept fumblings of a half-dead man, grasping for any bits of her life and fire.

The idea that Gulnar could have exposed him, related the incident to her lover—had she laughed as she'd told him? The way she'd struggled not to when he'd been so distressed after she'd taken her first full look at him...

And he'd thought Roxanne's revulsion had hurt! If his lack of hair had warranted such shock, he didn't want to think what knowing the full truth would do. Oh, he knew she was too kind, too versed in dealing with affliction to show revulsion. But he hadn't been about to risk it, had recoiled from her touch when she'd recovered from her shock.

He'd wanted to erase the moments of insanity, to return them to warm spontaneity, to keep her as a friend at least. She'd accepted his overtures, jumped on them more like, relieved. He should have been, too. He hadn't been.

Hearing her saying it hadn't mattered, then behaving accordingly, had torn him up! He'd wanted it over, but he wanted it to have mattered! He wanted the memory, the belief. To cherish. To sustain him.

One more thing he'd have to live without.

Dante made another detaining gesture to his fidgeting driver. "No need to get nasty, Fernandez. I may not be dying, but you're not catching me at my best either. Sorry if I was short but I just spent a very trying hour with Kauffman. If you've ever dealt with him, you know what I'm talking about. So, again, what's the emergency?"

Emilio's grudging consent to the enforced truce was evident. "It's not exactly an emergency..."

Gulnar stepped in front of Emilio, took over the situation. "I believe it is. Did you hear about last night's bombing?"

Dante shook his head, his chest closing. Gulnar's lips tightened. "Terrorists hit a housing complex in Fajana, the nearest town to Srajna. During initial triage we had one hundred and ninety-five cases, fifty-four of them urgent. I assisted in ten, including Dimitri Ivanov's. Dimitri is a GAO recruit, too, and he was injured when he went in to save a trapped family and the building collapsed completely. He had massive intra-abdominal bleeding and contamination from a ruptured spleen and large bowel and a split liver."

Dante's chest constricted more, at the atrocity, but equally with crushing relief. So this was what had kept her away! *Focus. It's not about you now.* "You performed damage control surgery?"

"Yes. All bleeding vessels have been ligated and solid organ sources of hemorrhage packed and the bowels stapled shut. After transfusions and irrigating the peritoneum he's been left open to guard against abdominal compartment syndrome."

He nodded, finally accessing his professional control. "Good. Definitive organ repairs should be in no less than 48 hours, after he's stabilized."

Gulnar frowned. "That's what his surgeon is saying. But Dimitri's face has also sustained massive injuries. Dr. Moya said he wasn't touching them, that an ocular blow-out fracture isn't an emergency, and anyway, that with Dimitri's precarious general condition, facial deformities and future functional problems were the least of our worries now."

"And you don't agree?"

Conviction and urgency warred on her exquisite face. "No! But since I'm just a nurse, my opinion carried no weight. So I need you—someone whose opinion they'll all accept. Only you can determine if my fears are justified before it's too late, and if they are, to do something about them."

A shiver of pride ran down Dante's spine. The faith lighting her eyes, firing her words and tone. She honored him with her belief. He had that of her at least.

Eagerness followed pride. Being of use when no one else could be, the challenge of restoring a damaged fellow human, the intricacies and surprises and problems entailed in surgery and getting through them, solving them, reaching the best possible outcome—it was all he lived for.

And it wasn't enough any more.

To prove how deficient it was, Gulnar stroked his

arm, her tenderness stroking his raw heart. "Was I out of line? If you're not up to this…"

He wanted to haul her to him, to drown in her life and caring. He crushed the urge in clenching fists. "I'm fine. Let's do this."

One second, everything existed. Emilio, his chauffeur, the busy street of the Azernian capital, the glaring sun, the pungent, dizzying scents in the air. The next, only she did. Gulnar. Passion and life and beauty incarnate. She reached for him, her supple arms going around him in a gentle hug that trembled with the effort not to give in to its inherent fierceness. Still afraid of hurting him?

Didn't she know she hurt him by just existing? Oh, hell, why was she hugging him? Why was she changing the rules again?

His confusion met Emilio's bleakness over her head and realization jolted through him. Emilio was used to this, to Gulnar making intimate overtures—and more?—to other men as he watched.

But why did he put up with it? If they were lovers? How could he?

Only one thing made sense. Emilio knew it was either accept it or lose her completely. And he'd chosen the lesser evil.

If so, Emilio had to be insane. Suicidal. Loving a woman and watching her throw herself at other men— that was the ultimate evil, utter devastation.

But if Emilio was that obsessed, that sick, what about Gulnar? Was that how she got her kicks? Was that what turned her on? That would make her even sicker.

No. No, she wasn't. Couldn't be like that. There had to be something he was missing, misinterpreting. Something crucial. Yes, this was it. He was too jumbled to know what to think, was jumping to the ugliest conclusions.

Gulnar kept her arm around his waist as she turned to Emilio. "Thanks for the ride, Emilio. I'll go back to the hospital with Dante. We'll meet you there."

Emilio gave Dante one long, tempestuous look then turned away without a word!

Gulnar turned up a bright face to him. Too bright. "Shall we?"

A malignant suspicion hit him, almost doubled him over. Carefully, he extricated himself from her caressing arm, took a step away, willing the ache clamping his body to ease, to let him breathe, talk. "What is this, Gulnar? Are you using me to punish your lover?"

She didn't look indignant, didn't voice any objections, just took his hand in hers, towed him to the black-windowed limousine. She slid in first, tugged him behind her and rapped out rapid Azernian to the driver. The man who looked more like a special forces agent than a chauffeur gave her an eager nod before she slid the sound- and sight-proof communicating glass shut. The next second, the car jolted forward and screeched away, tossing Gulnar backwards on the seat.

She sat there, looking at him, her eyes full and fathomless, rocking and pitching beside him with every violent turn the car made. He'd long sagged back on the seat, nerveless, his heart pounding. Then she just nestled into him.

Everything disappeared. Only the heat of her melting back into his flesh, a missing part of him that had been cleaved out and now restored. Only her head on his heart stopping it from erupting from his chest, her trembling arm around him keeping him from going to pieces. Only her softness and resilience and comfort and torment.

And he'd been surprised that Emilio would do anything just to remain near her? What would he himself do? Anything at all seemed a small price for anything with her...

Thoughts boiled over and evaporated.

He surrendered to her when she reached up, rained soft, tender kisses all over his face, doused him in contentment and heartache, in pleasure and sorrow. He wanted to weep with it all, crush her to him and reproach her for depriving him of her closeness and caring all those days. And now there'd be no more. He wouldn't even have the memories.

But she was giving him something now. He closed his arms around her, hoarding all he could of her for the empty existence ahead, his blood roaring thick and raw in his ears. He felt her breathless words reverberating in his chest, rather than heard them.

"You should know, Dante. Even if I were the kind of woman who'd play one man against another, I'd never use you—never you, Dante. What's more, Emilio isn't..."

She fell silent on a trembling breath, burrowed deeper into him. His heart tightened, his senses overloaded, his mind staggered. Feeling her, knowing it would be for the last time—too much! He squeezed her tighter, groaned his anguish and confusion. "Emilio isn't what?"

"Emilio isn't, has never been and will never be my lover." She rolled her head on his shoulder, raised her face up to him, close, real, overflowing with sharp and urgent emotions, her beauty and vitality piercing him to his core. "Will you be?"

CHAPTER EIGHT

"WHAT did you say?" Gulnar looked up at Dante as they entered Srajna General Hospital's intensive care unit. His night-dark eyes stared down at her, filled with storms—of what? Wariness? Reluctance? Temptation?

He said something again, and again it didn't register. She only heard the drone of his dark, rich voice over the hot, thick throb of mortification in her ears.

He'd been stunned by her offer. He'd stiffened then had sat there unmoving, his arms no longer taking her, containing her, just limp around her, his eyes closed and his breathing erratic, until they reached the hospital. She'd been so distressed by his reaction, and more by causing it, she hadn't even worked up enough coordination to move away. Sitting there, pressed to him, her every breath laden with his scent and agitation, her ears filled with the cacophony of their hearts' thundering, that had been her first glimpse of true torment.

But none of it mattered now. Dimitri. Concentrate on him!

It was Dante who tore his eyes away first, cleared his throat as he headed for their patient in ICU. "I just asked if 3-D X-rays are available for me to review."

Gulnar knew there weren't. "I've seen only regular X-rays. I don't think there is a 3-D facility in this hospital."

He wasn't impressed with the news. "Just get me every investigation and X-ray."

Gulnar turned to the senior ICU nurse, translated.

"I need this bed turned around." Dante stood back as his order was carried out. Gulnar stood beside him, horror sweeping her again at the sight of her dynamic young friend lying there like a gutted corpse, with his abdomen wide open and covered in plastic. And his face…

She was used to the worst. She'd had the worst. But when it was someone she cared about…! It was just another reminder not to care, never again.

What about Dante?

No. She could care about Dante. She did. So much— lord, so much. It was safe to care, she told herself, to let herself feel as deeply and as totally as she wanted. Then he'd be gone and she'd never know what happened to him.

Wouldn't that finish her off? Losing him when he walked away?

She no longer cared what happened to her after he was gone. She wanted whatever she could have.

Dante had taken his position at Dimitri's head, was giving his nightmarishly distorted face a long, assessing look. She could almost feel his diagnostic mind going into overdrive. Then he exhaled.

Gulnar winced. Please, let it be better than she thought. Let Dante, with his extensive experience, have a different, ameliorating opinion.

His gaze roamed over the rest of the ICU staff then back to her and Emilio, the only two English-speaking people around. "History, status and current measures?"

Emilio picked up the Azernian-written charts, looked at Dante. "He was in the debris for six hours before extrication. He's been intubated and on bag-valve mask with 100 per cent oxygen since extrication. On the last recording, ten minutes ago, pulse was 128 with irregular ectopics, BP 90 over 60 and oxygen saturation 90 per cent.''

Dante absorbed the facts, started to examine Dimitri's injuries by extra-gentle palpation, assessing the lacerations, pausing to feel the crackling of bone fragments and the give of undermined structures. ''GCS at the scene and all through until he was anesthetized?''

Gulnar looked over the rest of Dimitri's deficient case file, filled with reports from everyone who'd handled him from the bombing scene onwards. This hospital was totally unused to and unequipped to handle mass casualty situations. It had been chaos, with so much disorganized and missing.

She sifted through the messy notes, not finding any mention of Dimitri's Glasgow coma score.

She looked at Dante, exasperated. ''He was conscious at extrication, so he couldn't have been much less than fifteen at the scene. When I saw him immediately before surgery, six hours later, he was a six. Dr. Moya said that the debris pressure had stopped blood flow. Once it was lifted, abdominal bleeding increased, and he went into shock. He attributes Dimitri's deterioration to that.''

And how she wished he was right! His opinion that Dimitri wouldn't withstand the extended anesthesia of a lengthy reconstructive procedure, while on the surface conservative and pessimistic, was better than hers. Dante met her eyes. Seemed he shared her pessimism!

Her heart plummeted. Dimitri was too precious to lose. A rare and true source of hope around here. He made such a difference, so many people needed him. Like Dante… He just had to live—and live whole! But at the moment it looked he'd either deteriorate and die, or at best live deformed and disabled. The two possibilities skewered through her. Please, please.

Dante concluded his examination, looked at her. "Three walls out of four of both internal orbits are destroyed. Has there been no ophthalmological exam?"

Gulnar leafed through the reports. "Left eye only. Nothing mentioned about the eye's condition, just that there was no optic nerve cupping. I guess this supports Dr. Moya's diagnosis that there's no intracranial injury or rise in pressure."

Dante's massive shoulders rose in irritation. "It tells me nothing. For all I know, his right eye is lost, and his left eye is, too, by now. A lot can happen in fourteen hours. It's a sorry fact in mass casualty situations that seemingly non-life-threatening stuff gets overlooked and that as soon as a casualty looks stable, it's on to the next unstable one." Another exhalation. "Let's take a look at his eyes, and his brain through them."

A few words from Emilio to the efficient ICU staff brought the instruments Dante would need in seconds. He thanked Emilio, turned to her. "Gulnar, retract the lid for me."

Her heart blocked her throat, her stomach rebelled. She could take anything, had taken far worse than this, but somehow the idea of handling Dimitri's delicate, shredded flesh overwhelmed her. Just do it. Go to pieces later.

She took her position at Dimitri's head and applied extra-gentle, calibrated traction with the lid retractor, prying the swollen lids apart for Dante.

He first measured the intraocular pressure and examined the insides of the eyes for injuries. The eyes were also windows to the brain—changes in the optic disc supplied reliable information about any rise in intracranial pressure.

Dante pulled back on a sharp inhalation. "OK. First good news I've seen so far. Amazing, too. The eyes themselves are intact."

Gulnar heard Emilio's exhalation a few inches away from her ear. So he, too, had been holding his breath.

Dante raised his eyebrows at her. "Now I'd really like those X-rays."

Gulnar swung to the senior ICU nurse, who hurried out herself this time, came back in a couple of minutes handed Dante the films with a grim face. He thanked her in Azernian, made sure he caught the nurse's eyes, gave her a soothing smile. Gulnar's heart swelled.

How considerate he was. How tender. Oh, Dante. Still here, but already lost to her.

She clamped down on the tide of agony as he shook his head, looking at the X-rays. "Without 3-D X-rays or even CTs to visualize whole structure of the face and skull from all sides and in perspective, there's no way to see the injury in detail. But I guess this will have to do. When was this taken?"

"After surgery."

"Hmm. Emilio, Gulnar, come over here." Gulnar darted to his side. Emilio's surprise that Dante had included him made his movements slower. They both ended up hovering on either side of Dante. "Tell me what you see."

What she didn't see chilled her. She had no solid arguments, no clinical evidence to back up her belief. It was instinct. And no one had agreed with it. If Dante didn't either, her mind would be set at rest. She prayed he wouldn't. She exhaled. "Nothing much. But judgements based on plain X-rays tend to under-diagnose the extent of injury. Dr. Moya was adamantly against doing anything about the facial fractures. He said we could always have delayed reconstruction when Dimitri is out of danger.''

''But that's not your verdict, hmm?'' Dante probed.

''No!''

Dante released her eyes, pored over the X-rays again. And again both she and Emilio looked over his shoulders. ''Here—where you can't see it, but from my manual exam—is a pulverization of the naso-orbito-ethmoid bones constituting the whole mid-face. I thought that the frontal bone had been spared. It was only on palpation that I found out the posterior table of the frontal bone is also pulverized.''

''But how can the posterior table be fractured without the anterior one?''

Gulnar couldn't blame Emilio for being skeptical. The frontal bone, making up the forehead, was made up of two layers, an outer one and an inner one. The inner one almost never fractured if the outer one remained intact.

Dante shrugged. ''It happens. Rarely, but it does. And this misleading intactness probably accounts for your doctor's optimistic outlook. I wouldn't fault him too much. As you said, X-rays aren't useful in showing damage to the posterior table.''

''So this is why he has a normal fundus,'' Gulnar exclaimed. ''There is no rise in intracranial pressure because he's been leaking cerebrospinal fluid though the fracture all the time!''

Dante's lips twisted. ''And the reason for his deterioration is neither shock nor direct trauma to the brain, but a spreading infection. If he weren't sedated, he would have shown all signs of meningo-encephalitis.''

"Oh, Dimitri!" Of course. His brain was exposed to the elements through the fracture. But in that case... "Oh, God, Dante, he's been on massive post-operative corticosteroids—they can suppress immunity and promote infection!"

Dante glared at Emilio. "You didn't mention corticosteroids!"

Emilio glared back. "You're the surgeon. You should know what goes on post-operative medication orders!"

"Well, you can strike them out at once!"

Emilio strode to the ICU nurse, relayed the new orders, anger clenching his every muscle.

Gulnar interrupted their sparring, still thinking, all the pieces falling into place. "So there was no cerebrospinal fluid leaking from his nose because he'd been on his back, with his head extended backwards!"

Dante came to stand beside Gulnar, his eyes sweeping her with appreciation, respect. Yes, but there was more. Regret. Sadness.

He nodded. "Another misleading lack of evidence. You were absolutely right to suspect the worst, to get me here. It was uncanny how you felt his danger against all evidence."

She held herself rigid, swallowed a barbed lump of agitation and longing. "But why aren't the antibiotics doing their job now?"

"Not even broad-spectrum antibiotics are good at crossing the blood-brain barrier, at least not at the concentration needed to treat such an acute and severe infection. And, anyway, the area has very poor blood supply right now. Not much antibiotic-loaded blood is making its way there."

Everything made perfect sense, the explanation to her instinctive diagnosis. "Do you think there is a dural tear, too?'' If the frontal bone was fractured, it might have torn the outer brain covering attached to it as well.

"Very likely."

"If antibiotics aren't working, he could die of a cavernous sinus thrombosis."

Dante's eyes widened. A leap of admiration lit his eyes—he was impressed. This shouldn't be a time for such pleasure, but she couldn't help it. She craved his approval. And by tomorrow there would be no more of it.

"That's one of many things that could happen if his facial fractures are left untreated for any length of time. Which brings us to our catch-22 situation. We can't operate because he can't withstand the lengthy anesthesia and the multiple reconstructive procedures. We can't *not* operate because waiting would also kill him."

A feeling of impotence shuddered through her. What would they do now?

"So, Gulnar, where are those mini-plates?"

She blinked at his change of subject. "I ordered them the minute we arrived." He'd asked for the mini-plate and screw systems, the latest techniques to hold together small bone fragments. She'd thought he just wanted to have them handy, in case he decided to proceed with the reconstruction. "They didn't have any left, so they sent for them from Srajna's other main hospital."

"I just hope they make it by the time I need them to start stabilizing the bone splinters."

Her heart lurched. "You mean you will go ahead with the procedure?"

The corner of those lips lifted. "Let's scrub."

"Let's end this!"

Emilio's note of urgency rang in Dante's ears.

Dante knew he was pushing it, that Dimitri could stand no more. He still didn't know how the guy had held on that long—four hours of surgery and some of the most intricate and extensive reconstructive work he'd ever done. But there had been no way around it. On exposure, Dimitri's fractures had turned out to be far more catastrophic than even he and Gulnar had thought.

"Guerriero, just close him up. Finish this later!"

He couldn't. Dimitri was dead anyway if he didn't complete reconstruction. If not on the table now, then a week from now—maximum. There would be no other secondary surgery at a later date. It was now or never. He'd rather have Dimitri die in his hands as he fought for his life than die because he'd given up the fight.

But he could sympathize with Emilio's distress. It must have been too much for even him—a man who lived on the razor edge of violence and desperation, and by choice, seeing his buddy's face a dissected nightmare with Dante's hands and scalpels deep inside it. Emilio had reached his limit after Dimitri had flat-lined. What about Gulnar?

She was holding in her distress better than Emilio, murmuring encouragement to Dimitri.

Emilio was silent for a dozen heartbeats then hissed again, "Pulse 185, BP 70 over 40. We're losing him—again!" Emilio still didn't miss a beat of the flawless surgical routine they'd fallen into, handing Gulnar the cautery probe and preparing the next set of mini-plates.

"No, we're not." Gulnar's voice trembled as she cauterized and swabbed for Dante. Then it was time for the most important step, the frontal sinus ablation.

All through the first step of the procedure, Gulnar continued her murmurings to Dimitri between Dante's hushed requests for instruments and assistance. Then Dante sighed as he moved away from the surgical microscope. "Gulnar, I've removed all sinus mucosa. Sort through the removed bone slivers and fat pads, form me squares of one centimeter each. I will need them to obliterate the naso-frontal duct." It was where the infection was finding its way into the brain.

That took another ten minutes and Emilio announced again. "60 over 20. You've done the most important things. Anything else isn't life-threatening and we've already shocked him once. How many times does his heart need to stop before you end this?"

"Emilio!" Gulnar's warning mutter was almost inaudible. "Dimitri doesn't need to hear your doom-mongering!" Louder, she resumed talking to Dimitri, bolstering, tender—teasing. "You don't, do you, Dimitri? You're fed up with all that doom-and-gloom stuff, huh? You've held up all through this when everyone kept saying you wouldn't. You'll do this, won't you? You'll get through this so we can finish our chess game. I want to beat you and get one of your fabulous caricatures."

Dante's eyes darted from Gulnar's hands, as she helped him gain exposure of the central nasal bone fragments, to the monitors. Dimitri's pulse was slowing down, his blood pressure inching its way up.

It had to be Gulnar. The man had been hanging on all that time to please her. He just knew it. And he knew the feeling. He'd done it before.

"Good man. We're almost there," Dante murmured.

"Hear that, Dimitri?" Gulnar helped Dante as he reduced and stabilized the superior and inferior orbital rim fragments with mini-plates. "If—and that's a very long shot—you beat me, I'll set you up with Magdalene.

Yes, I know, and the good news is she feels the same. Now, all you have to do is get back on your feet…''

Dante ended up by reconstructing the nasal bone with a cantilever bone graft secured with a mini-plate. He finally tightened the last screw then sat back.

It was done. They'd put Dimitri's face back together. And not only was he still alive, he was stabilizing. And Gulnar was still murmuring to him, congratulating him, praising his effort.

Dante suddenly felt the need to communicate with him, too. He took the needle holder from the relaxing Emilio, picked up the threaded needle from Gulnar and smiled beneath his mask down at his patient. Dimitri would hear—feel his pleasure, his confidence. He hoped. ''Thanks Dimitri. It's been an honor fighting through this with you. We're closing you up now. And don't worry, I promise you the best esthetic result possible. Once the swelling and bruises disappear, the fair Magdalene won't even notice any scars.''

He felt Gulnar's eyes swinging up to him, hotter than a cautery probe. He wondered if they would leave scars.

He looked at Dimitri as he restructured his facial muscles and closed his skin. If it hadn't been for Dimitri, Gulnar would have come tomorrow on her usual morning visit to find Dante gone. He would have walked away with minimal regret, minimal scars. At least compared to now.

Now walking away from her would do more than scar him. Still, it was far better than what he'd suffer if he stayed.

What he'd make her suffer.

CHAPTER NINE

"DON'T you think I've suffered enough?"

Gulnar leaned back against a column in the scrubbing-gowning hall, struggling with the pain clamping her whole body.

Dimitri's nurse and anesthetist finished scrubbing for yet another procedure and cast another glance at her and Dante on their way out.

"What are you talking about, Gulnar?" His eyes darted to hers in the murky mirror above the wall-to-wall sink then darted away instantly.

"You're leaving me in suspense and it's killing me. Why don't you tell me what you are doing, Dante?"

"I'm dead on my feet, that's what I'm doing."

This wasn't exhaustion. She didn't know what it was or why. She didn't understand why he'd shut her out so completely, so suddenly. And she didn't have to. Didn't have time to. For whatever reason, he was just ending their liaison now, and not tomorrow. Tomorrow...

Knowing he intended to leave tomorrow had changed everything. When she'd thought she still had time with him, in any form, she'd laid off, given him his space, left it up to him to conduct their relationship. Even when he'd told her he'd return to the US as soon as he was healed, she'd still thought she had at least a month with him. But she had no more time and she had to be with him those last hours. She had to have tonight!

And he was pushing her away.

It hurt and humiliated her. It confused her and made

her want to curl up in the dark and never rise again. But it didn't matter. Nothing did. She had to have those hours.

"Gulnar, not only am I dead on my feet—"

"So let's get out of here. Let me take you away, you can rest and sleep—"

A harsh bark erupted from him. "Sleep? You think we'd sleep?"

"We'll do anything you want. I did promise anything before and I still do. Anything and everything we want. If you want to sleep, I want to hold you while you sleep."

He held up his hands and squeezed his eyes, an exasperated order for her to stop! "Gulnar, I'm walking out of here and checking into a hotel for the night. Then first thing in the morning I'm leaving. I'm never coming back. Do you understand this? You want a lover? It isn't me. There. That's your answer. Satisfied?"

"No. It doesn't make a difference, you leaving, not to me. And if you ever come back—"

"I won't. You've got to believe that."

Oh, she believed it. It was why she was desperate, why this was possible. "Then I want tonight, Dante. Don't you want it, too?"

His simmering sidelong glance said he did. But, then, he would want any female who stood there begging for anything with him.

Fine. She didn't expect an exclusive relationship. Wouldn't know what to do with one if she had one. Didn't want one.

She just wanted tonight.

He turned from her, bent down to lower his head to the sink. He held his breath and let cool water pour over his head.

The sight of water sluicing over his polished bronze skull thudded in her heart, behind her eyes, in her loins. An endless minute later, he straightened to his full height, water rivulets running down his head and neck, merging with the sweat darkening the green of his surgical scrubs.

Suddenly the space between them had disappeared.

"Gulnar…" His arms moved to push her away and convulsed around her instead, squashing her into his body. She melted immediately. The next second, he exploded away in disgust. "Dammit, Gulnar. Don't do that to me—not now."

"Later, then? My place? Your hotel?" *Say yes. Promise me tonight.*

"Gulnar!"

He dipped his hands under his scrubs, snatched his headscarf out of his pants pocket and in two violent movements wiped and wrapped his head, cornered, angry. "You're a hazard, Gulnar. For God's sake—you have no idea what you're asking for!"

He snatched the scrubs over his head, volleyed them into the laundry bin, exposing his massive chest and ridged abdomen. But even his beauty didn't distract her from the searing sight of his healing wound.

He turned away, heaving in steadying breaths. Her arms wound around his chest back to front, her fingers digging into his solid muscles, her lips quivering where the bullet had almost taken him from her. Her eyes brimmed with unspent tears, her body quaked into his precious flesh with all the horrific could-have-beens.

"Say yes, Dante."

"No." He tore at her hands, stumbled away and snatched open the locker they'd been given to keep their clothes in.

He put more distance between them, eyeing her as he prowled in slow, tense figure eights, buttoning his shirt. A caged lion taking stock of his tormentor.

Had she misunderstood it all? She'd thought their shared ordeal gave her some special status in his eyes, that he shared her attraction—however partially. It didn't seem so any more. She couldn't pretend any longer not to understand his withdrawal, his rejection. He didn't want her, not in any way, no matter how fleetingly. She was the one dishonoring and erasing anything that they'd shared.

Oh, hell—what had she *done*!

Then something even more crippling hit her.

"I just realized—I know nothing about you. I don't know whether you're married, or involved…" She stopped, shame shriveling her up.

His sharp inhalation suspended her agitation. The next second stretched out, the eternity before the verdict. Then he exhaled. "No. I'm not. Not any more. And I never will be again."

Air disappeared. She groped for it and it came, tearing, burning inside her chest.

He'd been married? Or deeply in love?

Of course he had been. He hadn't just emerged into existence the moment she'd lain eyes on him. He had to be in his late thirties, and…

It hurt to imagine someone, another woman, loving him, his body eager for hers, his eyes telling her what she meant to him, his heart racing, welcoming her.

It hurt even more that it had ended—and in pain? The thought of his pain, his loss was unbearable. What had happened? Had she died? Had he sworn off caring again, not wanting to be hurt, unable to lose again? Like her?

Was this why he went to areas of conflict, risking his life, daring death? Was it that his grief, still fresh and overwhelming, was prodding him for release, for an end to it all? And she'd intruded on the sanctity of his mourning.

Just leave him alone. Remember your own rule.

She never cared. Never got close. And Dante was probably the one man she shouldn't come near. The one man courting danger and death.

But it was too late. It had gone beyond caring, beyond closeness. It was beyond even what she had with Evraim.

And if it were only about her, she would have broken all her rules, invited devastation for that one night with him. But it wasn't about her—only he mattered now.

A nauseous claustrophobic sensation crushed down on her. *Just get out.* "I'll just go…" She got the words out somehow. "Goodbye, Dante…"

"Gulnar!" His imperative bark jolted her. She closed her eyes. No more humiliation, please! She ventured a look at him—and almost fell to her knees.

The burning intensity in his gaze! Did that mean…?

He prowled over to her, eased her back until he plastered her to the wall. He held her eyes until she whimpered. Then he said it. "Yes. *Yes*, Gulnar. Satisfied?"

She flung her arms around him, her tears flooding her cheeks. "Oh, Dante—not yet, not yet."

He crushed her mouth in a near-violent kiss. The pressure of longing was a heavy, viscous quicksand sucking her consciousness. He snatched his lips away, and his eyes. "Just remember—I did try to step back."

"I'll remember. And I'll try not to hate you for it."

His frown made it clear he'd misunderstood her. She could see him withdrawing in his mind first. "Hate you

for tormenting me, you idiot, for making me beg and
wait.''

"So we're back to calling me names, huh?'' There
was no humor in his voice or expression, just searing
emotion and sensuality.

"If you're fool enough to think I meant anything
else.'' She gasped, her knees almost giving out. He
stepped away from her, the driven look in his eyes slamming into her. He tugged her out of the hall past smiling
personnel. She ran in his wake, dazed, unquestioning,
quaking in anticipation.

He stopped only when they were at the end of a cor-
ridor housing the doctors' rooms.

One was open and there was no one inside. He tugged
her behind him as rushing personnel passed by and cast
them curious looks.

He locked the door behind them, looked down at her.
For answer, she wound herself around him, arms and
legs. He staggered with her until he opened the bathroom and spilled with her inside the shower cubicle, his
hand behind her head and his arm at her back taking
the impact against the tiled wall at the last second. They
remained like that for endless minutes, panting, their
bodies and gazes fused, exchanging memories, long-
ings, hunger—everything. She silently sobbed to him
what she couldn't say out loud, what she had no right
to say. *Dante, Dante, you're everything, my heart.* His
unending universes of inner beauty and strength and
tenderness said she was everything to him, too. And she
believed she was. For now. Until he left.

She brought his lips down to hers, sank into him with
all her love and despair. And he gave her back everything, then more, and more. More fervor, more intimacy, more abandon.

Suddenly Dante's groans doused her in dread. What if they were ones of pain? His injury—two weeks weren't enough for him to be back to normal…

Distressed, she unclamped him and attempted to regain her footing. He wouldn't let her, crushed her tighter to him, then shifted, taking their weight on his extended arms against the wall. His eyes detailed his pain and how his hunger overwhelmed it, negated it. Then he closed them, gritted his teeth. "I am going away tomorrow, Gulnar. Nothing will make me stay."

She bit him. His lower lip, his chin, his neck, silencing his mutilating verdict, frustration, grief, arousal sending her berserk.

Growls of pain, of voracity rumbled from his gut. He dropped her to her feet, tore her scrubs off her then swooped to his knees, yanked down her trousers. She wanted to help him, to be naked before him, against him, now, now, but she had no volition.

He put himself between her thighs, worshipped from calf to thigh to stomach. His hot breath, his voice, his passion scorched her flesh, She didn't obey him as much as she sagged in his grip completely. He nudged her thighs further apart, bent lower to bring them over his shoulders then heaved her up, her flaming hair streaming back, sliding upwards against the tiles, until she was straddling his shoulders. Then he buried his face in her.

A scream welled from her depths, too loud, too frenzied to form. The next one would have, but he reached out a hand to her mouth, caught it in his palm. She bit down, harder each time his tongue lashed her swollen, hypersensitive flesh. He was giving her no chance but to thrash every time he drove deeper inside her. But she just had to make him understand, tell him what would deliver her. Her voice wouldn't come. Her tongue filled her mouth and everything else in her, heart and body and soul, was swelling, overflowing. She managed a word, the only word that mattered. "You—you…"

He gave her one more hot, wet lash that almost had her blacking out then raised his eyes to her. Obsidian gems housing all his intellect and passion and virility, promising her what he had in store for her. "Yes, *amore*, me. You'll have all of me. You promised me anything and I promise you too, anything—everything."

She bit down hard on the heel of his palm as all her desperation detonated, crashing down through her, each convulsion wringing her tighter of every sensation her body was capable of.

And it left her feeling so empty that the last of her sobs were real distress, not the delirious weeping of release.

Her hands flailed on his head, gliding, memorizing, as he completed her pleasure, just enough pressure, enough insistence, making sure she had nothing more to want, to feel. He stopped only when there was no more, leaned his cheek on one inner thigh, rubbed his forming beard into it, sought her streaming eyes with his tenderly tempestuous ones, deepening the connection, heightening the intimacy.

It was undreamed of, caressing his face like that, experiencing his magnanimity. Her heart clenched an obsessive fist around the memory. It would never let go.

He let her down from his shoulders, held her to him, contained her, still fully clothed, absorbing her shudders, soothing her. "Shh, shh, *amore*—ah, *bellisima mia*—I've never seen or felt so much beauty, so much wonder…"

His words spread in her body and brain, balmy, corroding, had her whimpering to him again, incoherent, supplicant, desperate, "Please, *please…*"

He carefully propped her against the wall, a boneless heap. Then he rose and began to undress, his eyes giving her no respite. She needed none.

The ferocity in his gaze melded with the permeating gentleness of his essence, promised the violence capable of silencing the screaming tension, the cherishing that would express and assuage their need, on every level.

Seeing him standing above her, powerful, beautiful, had a backdraft roaring higher in her blood. She pounced on him, didn't know where she found the power, her need a ragged sobbing filling her throat.

He undid his buttons in a succession of frenzied motions—and it felt so slow! A growl of frustration erupted from her, her eagerness pushing him against the wall. She fell to her knees, in supplication, in ravenous wonder, took him between trembling hands and lips.

His surprise at the role reversal was short-lived, his surrender to her worshiping even shorter. He growled and hauled her up, fumbled her bra off and pressed his rough chest against her released, swollen breasts, abrading her stinging nipples. The sensation screamed down every tortured nerve, the very idea of the intimacy, of his need for it, inflaming her even more.

So he felt the same. It wasn't about physical release, but about merging, taking and being taken, finding that release with her, inside her.

Her heart still thrashed in her chest, demanding her instant addiction, his feel, his scent and taste…

"Take me inside you, *amore mio*—just take me…"

"Yes, yes, *yes…*" She strained in his arms, climbing higher, the legs clamping his steel buttocks flailing.

He flexed his mass and power, his manhood nudging her entrance, seeking, asking. Everything in her opened, accepted, surrendered. At last, Dante was invading her, completing her, holding her eyes as he eased his girth inside her, expanding her beyond her limits, letting her see every nuance of shocked wonder and pleasure transfiguring his magnificent face.

He thrust, full and hard, sought her depths. He found them, then further, where she'd never been touched, right through to her soul, filling all her emptiness and loneliness, ending her solitude.

All her nerves fired at once and she screamed. No— she wanted it to last for ever.

He withdrew, yet still clung to her, eyes and need and flesh, dominating her, surrendering to her. Then he rammed back into her. Her convulsions started from the furthest point he caressed within her body, spread in expanding shock waves, each building where the last just began to diminish, constricting her whole body around him inside and out. He withstood her storm, every shudder and tear and scream. Then he gave it back, plumbing a new depth inside her, impaling her to her heart, releasing all his agonized ecstasy there.

She drowned, thankful, replete, complete.

His tongue mated in moist, luxurious heat inside her still gasping mouth, twisting and turning in a languid, healing duel with her own. And there was rain, a warm, blissful shower cocooning them in an obscuring cascade.

A pungent scent enveloped them, familiar, cleansing. He was on his knees again and she was draped over him, her knees hugging his sides. He was still filling her, rocking gently as he worked the soap lather in easing, avid patterns over her back and buttocks. She slithered from him to kiss his face and neck and shoulders, took the soap and started her own worshipful painting.

So this was how it felt to feel, to love. To live.

Tomorrow, it would be over. But she still had the rest of tonight. Starting now.

She put her lips to his wound, prayed for him and gave thanks. Tonight would have to be her whole life.

CHAPTER TEN

"PLEASED with yourself, Guerriero?"

Dante turned slowly. He couldn't move any faster if his life depended on it. His life force had been drained in Gulnar, in their love-making. Only enough was left to keep him on his feet.

His swollen lips twitched, the imprint of her every tooth still shooting pained pleasure bolts to every erogenous zone. She'd bring him to full life, full frenzy again the moment he saw her.

She'd stayed behind with Dimitri, to talk to him some more, after he'd checked him, documented his short- and long-term post-operative care and allowed his removal from Recovery to Intensive care. Ten minutes, she'd promised. And no more, he'd insisted. He wanted every minute of the rest of the night and time was ticking by...

He met Emilio's bitter eyes and sighed.

So even war reaching their front doors hadn't overwhelmed the hospital staff's interest in the latest scandal. The amazing part was, he didn't give a damn who knew or who said what. He still didn't know what had come over him. He'd had no idea he had something like this in him, this blinding passion, this uncontainable hunger. On the last record, and presumably on the best of authority, he was a passionless bore.

I always needed more! But I tried excusing you, thought maybe it was your preoccupation with your ca-

reer. But you're just cold, *Dante! And now you'll lose interest completely and it isn't fair...*

Irony huffed out of him. If only Roxanne could see him now. Any hotter and he'd set the place on fire.

Emilio bristled. "Oh, laugh, Guerriero. Lick your whiskers. Don't think you're anything special though. You know Lorenzo Banducci, don't you? Gulnar went after him the same way, and for the same reason."

So she had gone after Lorenzo? Had Lorenzo succumbed to her as he had?

What kind of a stupid question was that? What man could resist her? And would Lorenzo have even tried? Of course he'd succumbed, taken all he could of her for as long as possible.

It shouldn't hurt. That was the past. And he had nothing to say, nothing he should feel, about her life or choices anyway, not in any tense.

He shouldn't. But he did. Feel. Too much. And he wanted to knock Emilio down for confirming his suspicions, for planting the corroding images of Gulnar with Lorenzo in his psyche, adding them to his other morbid imaginings.

But Emilio was in love with Gulnar, was hurting, too. He should feel sympathy for him if his pain was even a one-thousandth of his.

He didn't. Not in the least.

Though knowing he wasn't and would never be Gulnar's lover did remove him from the top of his hate list.

But Emilio seemed bent on venting some venom and he *could* afford to let him have some catharsis. He cocked his head at him, pretended interest. "And what is that reason she went after both me and Lorenzo—and not you?"

If she picked her men with certain physical criteria, he and Lorenzo shared almost all of them. Big, tall, distinctive, dark-skinned. Latin. But so was Emilio. Why had she excluded him from her list of possible conquests?

"I don't share the main criterion you both have in her eyes."

"What? Being surgeons?"

Emilio snorted. "Gulnar doesn't look at social status or money or perceived life-role importance."

Dante believed that. In her eyes, in her arms he was his basic self. She valued him, not what he did or was or had. She was the first one who ever had.

Emilio went on. "Gulnar doesn't have one shallow or covetous bone in her body. No, she has only one rule about the men she takes to her bed—figuratively speaking in your case. They have to be safe. And I'm not safe."

"Safe? What are you talking about?" An ugly suspicion detonated in his mind. "Heaven help me, Fernandez, if you've ever even *thought* of hurting her…"

Emilio waved him away in total boredom. "Don't be ridiculous, Guerriero. I don't hurt women, not in any way and not even if they drive me crazy and tear my heart to pieces like Gulnar has been doing for the last two years. Oh, OK, so she hasn't meant to, and it's my fault that she has, but anyway I'm not safe because I love her. She went after Lorenzo because she believed he couldn't care about anyone, not in an emotional, monogamous way. That made him safe. But even when he proved her wrong and fell for Sherazad, she still used him to drive her point home to me, to keep me away."

Gulnar had come between Lorenzo and his wife?

Hadn't cared that Lorenzo was in love, had seduced him, not caring if she would have wrecked his relationship, or broken another woman's heart?

No. He had to take Emilio's words with a *pound* of salt. A thwarted man wasn't the best source of information. And he had to trust the Gulnar who'd risked her life, who would have died for others. Who couldn't risk the possibility of his continued involvement and had almost walked away from him, making him lose his mind and every shred of inhibition. No. She wouldn't have done anything to deliberately and carelessly hurt another.

He scowled at Emilio. "But you just won't be driven away, will you? You just shadow her like a lost puppy, forcing your presence on her, trying to emotionally blackmail her into surrendering to your obsessive emotions!"

"I don't follow her around. We work together."

Dante barked an ugly laugh. "Oh, you *have* to be here? You can't ask for reassignment if you wanted? Or haven't you lost hope yet that she will respond to your persistence?"

Emilio drove his hands deep in his pockets, shook his head in resignation. "Oh, I know she won't. She's made it beyond clear. It'll probably take me going on an extended promiscuous spree to make her consider me."

"You don't have a very good opinion of her, do you? And you say you love her."

"I love her because, apart from this aberration, she is everything I *can* love. And because I can only presume to judge her if I lived anything like the life she has. And whatever happens to me, I'll never suffer a fraction of what she's suffered."

"Big of you."

"It took some doing, believe me."

Gulnar appeared at the other end of the spacious hospital reception area. Everything inside Dante rioted at the sight. Impatience tightened his head, his voice. He wasn't losing one second with her for anything. "Fernandez, if we're done here…"

"We are, Guerriero. Goodbye. Don't get yourself killed."

Dante had to laugh. "Don't you mean, *get* myself killed?"

Emilio half turned to him again, something like a smile shadowing his lips. "I don't want you dead, Guerriero. It's not your fault, what Gulnar is doing, what I'm feeling. And you're a hell of a surgeon and you do a lot of good. Believe it or not, you're one of the last people I'd like to see wiped out from this world."

"This *is* big of you. Seriously. I don't think I'd be so charitable in your shoes."

"Just pray you never are."

Dante's heart itched with regret. What a mess. In other circumstances, he would have liked to be Emilio's buddy. Not in this life, it seemed. He stopped Emilio, extended his hand. Emilio shook it in silence then turned away.

Two nurses stopped Gulnar's eager advance towards him. They kept looking over at him, interrogating her, no doubt, to judge from the blush radiating from her. He now knew it blazed all the way to her toes, spreading that incredible peach throughout the lush cream as he merged with her, watched her scaling satisfaction, writhing in his arms… *Distract yourself.* "Fernandez…" He cleared the covetous rasp from his tones, tried again. "You never told me what Gulnar finds so safe about me?"

Emilio half turned, shrugged. "Why don't you ask her?"

"I'm asking you. After all, you volunteered the information."

"Listen, Guerriero, I'm sorry. I shouldn't have done that. It just— After what happened all through the night I was raw, and I had one of my infrequent spiteful episodes. Just let it go. Tomorrow you'll be gone and there's no reason for us to be at odds."

"We aren't."

"We will be if I answer your question. When I walked up to you a few minutes ago, I wanted to hurt you."

"I noticed. But what makes you think whatever you have to say will hurt? I'm leaving tomorrow, if you haven't noticed." What was he doing? Why did he want to know this? Why was he pretending it wouldn't hurt?

Emilio gave him an assessing look. Then he shrugged again. "OK, maybe I'm wrong about you, maybe you're just one of those men who go through life with a scoring list. If you insist, she chose you because you share one of the things she chose Lorenzo for—she feels nothing for you, anything personal, that is. But your specific advantage is that you're leaving tomorrow, never to be seen again. You did notice how she pounced on you the moment you said you were leaving. It instantly made you safe."

It also made him feel sick. With rage and regret.

He shouldn't have asked. He should have left well enough alone. And he'd been worried she'd offered herself in desperation because he was leaving, then would later try to talk him into staying. He wouldn't stay, he couldn't, but he'd still wanted her to want him to, to feel something for him. As much as he felt for her.

He didn't want her to want him because he was a guaranteed one-night stand!

But he was going to be.

And knowing she wanted him to be should make leaving her in the morning easier. *Should...*

Emilio passed Gulnar on his way back and her face became that tense, apologetic mask. Dante almost resented Emilio again. The guy should disappear from her world, never to return. He had no right to be burdening her with his emotions.

As soon as Emilio had passed Gulnar, she ran to him and his heart expanded so hard his chest almost burst with it. She threw herself in his arms and consumed his will and reason.

No. He would walk away. There was no changing that. And she didn't want him to stay. That would keep him on target—on time. No lingering, no regrets.

He almost laughed at this, harsh and shearing. No lingering maybe. No regrets, no way. Nothing but regrets would remain.

He swayed into her, huddled around her as she burrowed into his side and whispered into his chest, "C'mon—let's get out of here. I need you all to myself for the rest of the night."

The rest of the night. He had to cram a lifetime into it.

"Welcome to my humble abode."

Gulnar's bright invitation thumped in Dante's chest. His eyes roved around the dank, dark room. It was just one room, couldn't be more than ten by ten feet, with just one splintered door opening into what had to be the bathroom. An oppressive shade of green, rendered even more so by the accumulated dirt of probably decades without a paintbrush, enveloped them. Occupying the wall with the prison-cell-like grid window was a battered loveseat. He'd seen far better-looking couches in junkyards. Three outfits, all trousers and shirts of unmatching colors, like the stuff he'd seen her in all through the last two weeks, hung from nails on the cracked wall. A narrow, unmade bed leaned against the other wall, rickety, another piece of junk. The wooden floor was decayed and caved in.

Was this what GAO gave their volunteers? The people who risked their lives for others every day? Below nominal pay and subhuman accommodation? Was this what she called home?

She turned at his silence, followed his stare. "Sorry about the mess. I don't really have time to clean."

Clean *what*, for heaven's sake? This place's only hope for any semblance of restoration was to be torn down brick by brick and rebuilt from scratch. "Is this where you live?" He was angry. Enraged.

"Oh, no. It's just temporary." That was better. If not by much. Just the thought that GAO was letting her stay in a place like this, no matter for how short a time— his blood boiled again. "I came to Srajna on a very short assignment, mostly to give a course in mass casualty triage in Srajna's General Hospital. I made use of being here and searched out an old acquaintance of mine, a woman who used to work with GAO, providing food supplies to us. She asked me to meet her where she worked—and the rest, as they say, is history."

So that was what she'd been doing with the Azernian hostages. He'd never even asked. He'd forgotten to ask. Forgotten everything else, too. Whenever he laid eyes on her, everything ceased to matter, to exist. But not now. This was about her, something she was suffering. And it was intolerable. "Short assignment or not, they shouldn't have made you stay in a place like this, in a neighborhood like this."

She snapped the elastic band out of her hair, shook out the fiery waterfall. He heard a roaring like an oncoming train in a tunnel. What were they standing around here talking for? Her answer reminded him. "Oh, it's very safe. As far as anything can be safe in a world of booby-trapped cars and rigged municipal buildings, that is! And this isn't far below our usual accommodation level really. GAO has been falling on harder and harder times financially. Every available cent goes for all the stuff that keeps our operations running, and accommodation ends up getting the short end of the stick. But I'm used to it. I think I'd feel lost in anything more luxurious."

Would his head blow up with frustration? "*A refugee camp* is more luxurious!"

She chuckled at his words. "Believe me, it isn't, and I should know. I lived in one for five years. Here I at least have four walls and a door. And a bathroom!"

Something searing and viscous burst in his chest. Had his heart ruptured with impotence and oppression? It might have. Gulnar, his unique, indomitable beauty. Terrorized, degraded, destitute. Used to it and taking it in her stride—no, almost as her due, what life owed her. Expecting nothing better, as if it was no worse than she deserved. Oh, *God.*

"If you'd rather go to a hotel…" Her gaze anxiously scanned his face. She must have misunderstood his chaos for she stopped, squeezed her eyes and swung away to make a silent yet eloquently furious self-berating gesture. "Of course you would. I don't know what I was thinking, bringing you here. I guess I didn't want to lose time searching for a hotel, checking into one…"

Wet heat detonated behind his eyes, corroded twin paths down his cheeks. He lunged after her, caught her around the waist from the back, his arms crushing her into him. Trembling, gasping, he carried her to the bed, pushed her down and covered her. He wanted to shield her, contain her, squash her into him, hide her inside his body.

She squirmed beneath him, panted, "Dante, if you don't want to leave, then let me loose—let me, please…"

He opened his mouth on her pulse, seeking every confirmation of her existence and life and something bitter mingled with her sweat in his mouth. His tears. Or hers? "Next time, *tesoro*. Next time."

He wanted to tear her clothes off, but couldn't. She didn't have much to replace them with. He could give her all she needed. Oh, how he wanted to lavish everything he was and had on her…

His dexterous fingers were useless with emotion, snarling over undoing her shirt buttons. She was trapped beneath him yet going a better job than him. He pulled back, freed her from that memorized khaki shirt. She'd aroused him with it during the hostage situation, beyond his comprehension. He remembered his confusion about her keeping it on in the deadly heat. And now he'd seen her without it, he knew why she'd kept it on. Her semi-naked body would have driven the militants to extremes, would have driven them beyond caution, beyond survival even to get their hands on her body, to spend their sick lust…

A sob tore out of him, came out a roar of rage and sorrow. His blood was congealing. He had to protect her, to honor her, to give her anything she needed. But how could he ever do that when he wouldn't be there for her? If not tomorrow then soon anyway? He just had to find a way. He would…

She half turned in his arms and they snatched feverish kisses and caresses, gasped and groaned and writhed together in a tangle and somehow ended up naked. He turned her again, lay over her back, clamped himself around her, arms and legs. Protecting, warding off the world. She squashed herself against him, demanding him, giving him herself. "Dante—darling, just take me… Don't hold anything back!"

He took her. Gave her himself. Held nothing back. His roar harmonized with her moan as he invaded her, as she consumed him. He had to plunge deeper into her being, surrender further. Had to give her what she was desperate for, all he had to give, his passion, full release and succor.

His rhythm built, her cries rose—and then it all detonated. The annihilating ecstasy that would silence agony, assuage need, wipe out existence.

They convulsed together until their cries were of desperation for the pleasure to subside, the keening edge to blunt. He poured himself into her in burst after draining burst, wished he'd disintegrate inside her.

With the last pulse of pleasure he collapsed on top of her, drove her into the lumpy mattress. A relieved sound poured out of her when his full weight bore down on her. He understood it. The same sound was welling out of him at feeling her precious body cushioning him, completing the intimacy, anchoring the magic of what they'd just shared.

They didn't speak. There was nothing to say. They just rested, regained their breath then loved again. And again.

Then it was dawn and they hadn't slept. The first bleak ray of light came through the grid window, portending the end. Gulnar was draped over him, her lips working patterns around his wound. She suddenly spoke, her satin voice cracked and thick with her abandon in his arms. "Sorry I brought you here. This place...really stinks..."

He dragged her up, swallowed her faltering words. "I've had all-luxuries suites, Gulnar. Color coordinated, silk sheets, incense burning, lights of a hundred artfully arranged candles, mirrors, water beds, music—and none of it matters. Only you, experiencing you, your mind-blowing beauty—your desire, feeling you, just the luxury, the magic of your pleasure and fire and life, Gulnar. I've never known such hunger, never had such satisfaction then such desperation all over again. *Never*, Gulnar..."

She turned in the curve of his still trembling body and murmured in his chest, "I'll just sleep till..."

She didn't complete the sentence.

Till what? Till he left?

He could tell she didn't really fall asleep. But she was giving him a way out without a confrontation. Without a goodbye.

He took it. At eight a.m., when he finally mustered enough will and co-ordination to move, he slipped from around her. It felt as though he'd snatched off his skin. He stood there dressing, his eyes hot and wet as he looked at her, twisted in the bed sheets, voluptuous, innocent and the one and only thing that mattered. Nothing else would matter again.

He paused at the creaking door, wished she'd call him back. That she'd at least sob in her pretense of sleep, give him a sign she wished he'd stay...

What was he thinking? That she'd want him to stay so he could tell her he couldn't? Soothe his torment and add to her suffering? But she wasn't suffering—was she...?

Just get out of here!

He did, stumbled out of the derelict building and into the ugly light of a new barren Azernian morning, truly lost for the first time in his life.

Where did he go from here? And why?

He'd just left all reason—and all his reasons—up there in that squalid room.

Gulnar held back the storm of misery until his footsteps faded. Then it pummeled its way out of her, slamming her around the bed, shaking her bones apart. She'd thought she'd wept, known desperation and loss before.

She'd known nothing.

Dante. Dante. Gone. Over. It was all over.

CHAPTER ELEVEN

"It's all over, Gulnar. All the pain and loss."

"You're back!"

"Yes, I am, Gulnar. I couldn't stay away."

"Oh, God, Dante. Say that again…"

"Did you hear what I said?"

Gulnar blinked. Her eyes were open and she did see the woman in front of her. The woman who'd just yelled at her.

Oh, hell! She was daydreaming again. Lost in her impossible fantasy. For thirty-four days now, ever since Dante had left, it had been the only thing that had kept her functioning, the escape she'd needed to salvage her sanity. Or so she'd told herself. If she was sinking into it now, involuntarily, unable to resurface from it, this could be serious. Would she soon fail to differentiate between fantasy and reality, take refuge in her delusions on a permanent basis?

She was still hearing his voice over the woman's tirade, soothing her, promising her he'd stay, at least somewhere in her life, that he wouldn't disappear completely.

Face facts! Dante had disappeared. He'd walked out of her arms that morning and had vanished off the face of the earth. No one knew where he'd gone. No one had even reported seeing him anywhere on his way out of the region. There were no records of his movements anywhere. And there should have been, with him such a well-known figure at the moment.

Had he really existed or had she been having an impossibly detailed and vivid psychotic episode all the time? Had her mind finally caved in, taken enough horrors and losses and desperation and decided to find itself a way out? Created her a man beyond her dreams, a passion beyond her imagination?

But why had it also given her grief beyond her endurance? If it had, then her mind must really be diseased. To introduce him to her in such a horrific scenario, to make him so perfect, yet so unattainable, so that losing him would be a far worse trauma than anything it had invented him to escape.

No. To her regret, her mind was still sound. And it would remain so, so she could suffer and know it. Dante and the two weeks of their relationship, the night in his arms were real. Only real life was that cruel. She knew…

"Don't you ignore me!" The woman was screaming now, and that catapulted Gulnar back, plunged her into the dreary reality that was her world. All around her was the dismal Sredna refugee camp populated by over two hundred thousand Badovnans. A scene from a recurring nightmare.

She'd been here before, with Lorenzo and Sherazad. She'd watched their love blossom, had misunderstood it at first. But they were together now, strong and secure in each other, with a baby on the way. And she was alone—for ever…

Focus! Before that woman goes for your throat!

"Madam—I was just a little distracted. It was an eleven-hour drive getting here, and I'm exhausted. If you'll please repeat what you said…"

"We all know you're one of the doctors who saved the Azernian hostages." Well, well. News traveled widely. "How dare you come here when you side with the people who put us here?"

Gulnar tried her best placating tone. "First, I'm not a doctor, just a nurse. And I'm with GAO, and you know we help people in need regardless of their nationalities or political beliefs. I was here a year ago. If you don't remember me, maybe someone else who's been here longer will."

"You saved Azernians and killed Badovnans!" the woman frothed. "You could have killed one of our brothers or husbands and now you're coming here pretending to help us…" Then she lashed out at Gulnar, her fist catching her on her ear with all her strength.

A thunderclap exploded in Gulnar's brain and everything came back in an avalanche. The whole hostage situation, the last minutes, Dante standing there, drawing the rebels' fire, protecting everyone, Dante turning around, seeking her eyes, the shocked knowledge that he'd been shot surfacing in his…

"You listen to me! You listen to me, all of you. I killed a monster and I don't care what nationality she was or whose sister or mother she was. She killed unarmed people before my eyes. She was going to kill the man I love. I would have shot my own sister in the same situation. Do you hear me?"

"C'mon Gulnar—it's not worth it…" Emilio had taken her gently in his arms.

"*No!* They have to hear this!" She struggled away from him, swung around to face her nemesis. The woman was glaring at her. "You think you have license to hate and kill because you've been wronged? You think you're the only one who's been wronged? You think your way is the only way? It isn't! I spent years in a camp worse than this one, an outcast and an orphan, and I didn't get out of it bent on punishing those who put me there, along with their allies, and their loved ones, and neighbors, and anyone who didn't side with me. I came out to help those who got trampled like I was. And that includes you!''

"I'd rather die than take your help!'' the woman yelled, and spat on the ground.

"Is this how you're raising your children? To bring on you decades of war and displacement? Don't you understand that by embracing vengeance and sanctioning terrorism, you are perpetuating your own suffering?''

"Enough, Gulnar.'' Emilio placed his bulk before her, blocking her from sight. He turned to the crowd. "OK, people, now's the time to make this clear. If you don't want us here, just say so and we'll leave.''

One of the men came forward, late fifties, balding. "We're sorry for all of this, sir. We appreciate GAO and everyone who works for them. I remember you from the last time you were here. And the lady. Tatiana is just overwrought, since both her brother and husband died recently in the fighting.''

"Do we have your word nothing like this will happen again?'' The man nodded. Gulnar remembered him now. He was one of the camp leaders. Emilio almost lifted her off the ground before she said anything more, dragging her with him in the direction of the tent they'd erected as soon as they'd arrived.

They didn't reach it.

A supply truck came hurtling towards them, screeched to a skidding halt among a storm of dust right beside the tent. The passenger door swung back on its hinges before it stopped. Then he jumped out and everything vanished. Dante!

Dante!

She froze.

Was her mind playing tricks on her? Was it summoning his image to rescue her from the frustration? She blinked and he remained there, motionless, his eyes on her. Only her. Fierce, full. Then he began to walk towards her, his steps slow, filled with his effortless grace. Illusion or not, she'd bolt towards him. Something anchored her. Emilio's grasp.

"Take him to the tent, OK? I'll give you an hour, and then we'll have to start setting up our operation."

Her dazed gaze went to Emilio's face, his words replaying in her mind. How kind he was. How she wished it could have been different. It couldn't. She'd pushed him away, afraid of caring, of losing. But she now knew she'd been able to only because he wasn't the one. When it was, fear had had no say, no place. Giving her heart had demanded no safety nets, no conditions.

Emilio smiled at her and she saw it. Something new. Acceptance, ease. And something gone. That sickness of longing that had long tainted his soul. *God, please, let him be cured. Let him find the one who'll be his own, for better or worse.*

She kissed his hard cheek. "Thank you—my friend!"

He moved away and she swung round to Dante. Oh, Dante. Her indescribable Dante. How she loved him. *Loved* him. And he was here. *Here.*

But why had she even assumed it was her right to run to him? Did she think he was here for her? He had ended it before it had started. He'd said when it would end, hadn't bothered to say why. And she'd sworn she'd never cling to him. Never ask him for what he wouldn't give in total freedom. And why would he want to give her anything? What was she but another woman from an underprivileged world whom he'd met in catastrophic circumstances and who'd given him fleeting sexual relief?

The left side of her face throbbed with the woman's blow. The rest of her followed suit, with futility.

She stopped a foot from Dante, looked way up into his beloved face. He had another hideous scarf around his head and more lines to his face. Had to be the harsh sunlight.

Throw yourself in his arms anyway. Beg him for anything, for any length of time.

No. You've already done that once. It's up to him now.

"Dante…" She escaped his unfathomable gaze, made a gesture, preceded him into the tent. She turned to him the moment he followed, tears rising. *Keep it light.* "You always know how to make an entrance."

His eyes dropped to his feet, studied the large sneakers with great absorption. Then he exhaled. "Is that praise or criticism?"

She huffed a failed attempt at a chuckle. "You're no slouch in the exit department either. So, what brings you here? Passing through, looking for crises to defuse? You missed today's crisis by mere minutes." She brushed her hair aside, rubbed her face, winced.

He took four storming steps towards her, stopped, his fists clenched. Then he gently removed her hand, replaced it with his, examining her. She saw murder in his eyes. It did have shape and color. "Who did this? One of the men here? Emilio? Tell me who!"

"So you'll beat the hell out of them?" She chuckled for real this time. He might not feel anything special for her, but he would still defend her to the death. Her shaved, fasting knight. "No, thank you, Dante. I just gave a hysterical speech about violence not being the answer." It was no use. She was too weak. She pressed her cheek into his beloved palm. "And Emilio? How could you even think it? Emilio is my dearest friend. My longest lasting, too."

His fingers, gentle, soothing, ran over what she assumed was the outline of a spectacular bruise. "He'd like to be more than that."

"And he went into a rage and hit me because I'm not co-operating?"

His eyes darted away, his jaw clenched. "You're not?"

She nuzzled his hand like a cat. "I already told you I never will. It's just not possible." His eyes swung to her, the fierceness rekindled, doubled with…uncertainty? About her words? No, she knew he'd always believe her—so was it about Emilio? "Oh, Dante, Emilio is one of the good guys. The best guys." His eyes did that weird glowing thing again, fire in their depths. Jealous? *Oh, please, let him be.* She was self-indulgent enough to want him to be, however little, for whatever reason. She'd take his attention any way she could get it. "It was a woman, by the way. Contesting my right to be here after I'd killed fellow Badovnans. You'd probably upset them even more, being the Azernian national hero that you are."

"That *is* a concern I've discussed with camp leaders at length. They assured me no one here supports Molokai and his criminal methods and everyone is just thankful to have us here. Clearly not everyone is, though. Hopefully you dealt with your confrontation diplomatically?"

"So you missed the part where I told you I hysterically lectured them?"

And he laughed. Full and deep. Peal after peal of virile laughter. "Ah, Gulnar, you unpredictable *bambola*!"

All her artificial lightness drained. It was just too painful.

He took her fully in his arms, anxiety blazing from his eyes. "What is it? Are you in pain? Feeling dizzy? What did she hit you with?"

"Just her hand. But let me tell you, that woman forges swords with her fist." It was spectacular seeing his unwilling smile defeating his frown. Then he kissed her, exploratory touches, tasting her, keeping his eyes open, asking her. Her answer was instant and total surrender. A profound sound rose from his gut, filled her, shook her, relief and hunger made audible. Then he devoured her.

Dante. Dante. Being without him had to be worse than death.

"Gulnar, I couldn't stay away…"

Oh, God, no! He was saying the lines she'd imposed on him in her fantasy. Was she hallucinating again? Had it all been a delusion again?

She snatched herself from the hands running over her in a fever, groped all over his face. He caught her hand, took it to his mouth, kissed and suckled.

She shoved her hand harder between his teeth. "Bite me!"

His laughter rang out again, his eyes melting with indulgence. "You're way beyond unpredictable, *amore mio*." And he bit her. Her whole body jerked with pleasure, with the debilitating relief of homecoming. He was really here.

*   *   *

Dante couldn't believe he was really here and holding her again. It had taken all his courage, and all his weakness, to risk coming back.

He breathed her in, angled his mouth against hers. Then he sank. He felt life rush through him, passion cresting in dark, overwhelming waves, crashing inside him. Magic. And love. More. Adoration and beyond. His Gulnar…

"We have an hour!"

Her moan reverberated inside him, made no sense. He raised his head, gasped, "What?"

"Emilio gave us an hour."

He did, huh? Well, well. "And do you want to devour me, like I want to devour you in that hour, Gulnar?"

Her eyes rivaled the sea in its most violent rages, slamming him with her answer. Then she said it. "Yes."

He hauled her back to him and she tore at his scarf, running grasping hands all over his head, his back, her kisses deluging him.

He snapped his head back again, cupped her face with both his hands, his thumbs smoothing her lips, catching her fervent kisses. He wanted to feel them all over him, cherishing and consuming. But he had to do something first. Something ugly, but the one thing that would make this possible. "Rules. Rules first, Gulnar. You may tell me to go to hell when you hear what I have to say…"

Her eyes stopped caressing him, her arms slipped off his body, then she stepped away, removing her face from his grasp and all warmth from his body.

It was spectacular, the way she turned off. Even more

the way it hurt, the way he'd come to depend on her. Being deprived of her focus, even momentarily, almost wrecked him.

His jaw clenched, suppressing the pain as she moved away from him and shrugged. "I know what you'll say. This is temporary. Anything else?"

She was OK with it, then? She really felt nothing beyond sex? It crippled him to know that, but it was for the best. Her best. It was what had made returning possible. He shouldn't wish for more. Should pray there was no more.

"I've taken the helm at the Sredna camp operation. I'll be here for two months. And I want to spend every possible free second soaking up your nearness, your eagerness—drowning in you, Gulnar."

"Then we say goodbye."

He nodded, the movement slow, hard. "It's the only thing to do. I don't do commitment, and you don't either. Two months, then I'll move on."

She looked away, stared into space. "What if it burns out way before that?"

Dante's lips twisted. He hadn't thought of that, had he? He'd thought she'd barely be able to tear herself away at the end. Like he would. Was she telling him there was a strong possibility she'd be sick of him inside a week?

Something tore inside him. He gritted his teeth. Just another blow to endure, to survive. He'd take that week. "No strings, Gulnar. None. You have enough, just walk away. I won't even ask what's wrong, won't try to persuade you to extend our time together."

"This applies to you, too, of course."

Would he ever have enough of her? With her taste and essence and love embedded in his cells and echoing

in his mind, there was no way in hell or on earth he'd
ever have enough of her. But he'd have no more than
the two months. They would have to be enough. "We
both have total freedom and there will be no recrimi-
nations whatsoever when either one wants to end the
affair."

He waited for her to say something, felt the slow
constriction of his heart, the vice that would keep on
tightening until it cut it in half.

Maybe he shouldn't be doing this. What if he
couldn't walk away as he intended? He'd failed once
already. He'd come back and was excusing it by telling
himself he'd walk away again. What if kept doing that?
Inventing wilder schemes every time to be with her?
What if she pushed him away and he clung?

No, he wouldn't. One reason would always remain
that would hold him back, keep him away. This time
for ever.

She remained silent, her eyes downcast, and suddenly
a horrible suspicion hit him. What if she just wanted
one more night—less, that "hour"—and that was all?
"Stop me any time, OK? If the night we shared doesn't
mean the same to you as it does to me, if it wasn't the
best sex of your life, the most magnificent thing that
has ever happened to you, if you don't stay awake at
night reliving…aching for every moment and touch and
sensation of our love-making…" Her magnificent eyes
widened. Because she was the one used to being forward? He went on, "If you don't walk around daydreaming about me, if you're not going crazy not having me, just tell me to go to hell. We'll just work
together, no harm done."

It was only when tension almost had him knocking
down the central tent pole that she let out a tremulous
exhalation. "You feel all that and you'd just get it all

under control and work with me as only a colleague, no problems?''

''There'd be problems. Big problems. But they'd be mine. You don't have to worry about them. I promise I wouldn't even look at you longer than necessary.''

Oh, the way she looked at him. What did it mean? Was she going to laugh in his face now? Was it possible…?

Her words braked his roiling thoughts. ''Our night together was the best thing that ever happened to me, Dante—period. And the only real sex I've ever had. If you only knew how much I want you, you'd probably run.''

He laughed. His first laugh of unbridled joy. Ever. And he wanted to weep, too. He pulled her back into his arms, slowly, savoring the heart-aching feel of her filling them, life ebbing back into him with each inch of contact. ''I'll only run to you. Show me how you want me, give me all you got, *amore mio*.''

''The hour is ticking by.'' A quivering smile lit her magnificent face, lit up his world as one hand dipped into his shirt, caressed his healed wound.

He captured it, buried his grateful lips in the soft, strong palm, then he nipped it. He caught her cry of pleasure in his mouth, poured all his longing into her eager lips. ''Gulnar, I missed feeling you, tasting you—missed you. I can't wait, *amore*. I just want to take you, hard and fast, just taking the painful edge away. Then we'll have the rest of the hour, all the time we have together for slow and thorough and world-shattering. What do you say?''

An unrestrained giggle of pure delight burst from her lips as she tugged him back hard to her. ''I say if you don't live up to your promises right away, I may hurt you!''

CHAPTER TWELVE

"DOES this hurt?"

"Yes!"

Gulnar removed her hands, stood back.

She assessed her patient again. Thirty-three, underweight, pale—but not exactly the paleness of anemia, at least not only of anemia, which most of the camp inmates suffered from anyway.

They'd been treating hundreds of cases with gastrointestinal complaints, which was also expected in their nutritional and hygienic state. Diarrhea, malnutrition, all sorts of dysentery. She shuddered again as she recalled the desperate time when a cholera epidemic had swept the camp during her time with Lorenzo and Sherazad. Even with the hundreds of ailments they treated per day, even a few dozen cases of typhoid, at least there was no true epidemic.

Most patients had been straightforward cases. This one wasn't. From the moment he'd walked in, he'd been so inconsistent, so whiny, she had at first suspected he was a hypochondriac. He complained of too many unrelated symptoms, and when she'd examined him, he'd hurt everywhere.

Her mind raced, unwilling to dismiss him as a malingerer. *Think!*

She put her hands back on his concave abdomen and palpated gently. He moaned with each dip. But it was when she palpated his liver that his moans were louder. She ventured a deeper dip and he keened. She disregarded his squirming and dipped deeper and… Hmm. The liver consistency wasn't as it should be. She could only feel it now she'd stopped being intimidated by his thrashing around.

OK, if she dismissed his accounts of hurting down to the last phalanx of his little finger, this looked like a lead. That and that yellowish tinge to his skin. She couldn't be sure it wasn't their horrible lighting giving him that cast, so she took off her glove and contrasted her hand to his color.

No. Yellowish. Definitely. All right. Now to look for other confirming signs. He was coughing, had a very low-grade fever and wasn't eating because he always felt full. He said he passed strange "stuff" in his stools, had vomited it once, too. And he was itching madly. She'd thought he had an infestation at first, was starting to get sympathetically itchy, but now…

This could be something that would need Dante's intervention.

And as usual, like it had been all through the past five weeks, whenever she thought of him, he was there. He was there all the time.

He'd stepped out of their shared examination tent to perform a quick procedure in the surgery tent, had only needed their anesthetist, Sam Hiller. He'd been gone thirty minutes. And now he was back, walking into the tent, snatching her heart with pride and joy. He was hers. For now.

He met her eyes, reconnecting with her, their escalating intimacy there for all to see in his. Her patient let out an exaggerated moan the moment he saw Dante.

"Any help?" Dante gave her a quizzical glance.

"Please!"

He snapped on fresh gloves and only then noticed

that she had one of hers off. "Tell me you haven't touched him without a glove! If you have, disinfect your hands right now. Don't bring them anywhere near your face until you do! Hell, disinfect your face."

"Hey take it easy—"

"*Do it*, Gulnar! The guy has jaundice and, until we know how he got it, I have to assume he's infectious!"

My. Just one look and he reached the diagnosis she'd agonized over!

"I didn't touch him, darling. I was just contrasting the colors of our skin to decide if he does have jaundice."

"Well, he does. And humor me, OK?" He looked over his shoulder to the other exam station. "Who's behind that curtain?"

"It's Helena." She was their only Badovnan nurse.

"Tell her to do it, too, just in case."

She signed in resignation, did as she was told. She came back from Helena's station, sticking her tongue at him. "Over-protective despot!"

"And you love it." Her heart quivered her consent. She loved everything he did and was. She knew he knew it, saw it, felt it. His eyes told her he did, before he disengaged his teasing, tenderly devouring gaze from hers and smiled down on their patient. "Mr. Khurdi, isn't it? Nice to meet you. Sorry for the lack of direct communication." The guy must have understood something for he gave him a nodding grimace. Dante tilted his head at Gulnar. "History?"

She recounted Mr. Khurdi's complaints and her findings. Dante nodded and started conducting his own examination. "Hmm." He finally stepped away, took her aside and raised one eyebrow at her. "Your diagnosis?"

"Are you testing me, darling?"

"As if you need a test, *amore*!"

Her heat shot up with mortification. "I needed one yesterday when I couldn't diagnose that ectopic pregnancy!"

She shuddered, remembering the emergency surgery that had followed her delay in diagnosis, the hemorrhage, almost losing the woman and having to sacrifice one Fallopian tube when the patient's other one was obliterated by adhesions.

It had been a bone-melting relief when the woman had burst into tears of thankfulness on being told! She had five children and had been going to pieces with the thought of any more. There hadn't been consistent birth-control measures since she'd come to the camp and she'd had two unwanted pregnancies during that time. One had resulted in twins.

"It was very misleading," Dante said dismissively. "With her history of ulcerative colitis, severe abdominal pain usually means a recurrent attack of inflammation. And you did diagnose it in the end, you just took longer to sort out the differential diagnosis."

Her lips twitched. "You're too good for my ego."

He gave her a look of genuine perplexity. "It baffles me that you don't have a planet-sized ego. You're phenomenal, *amore*!"

Pleasure at his praise spread through her as he picked up Mr. Khurdi's chart and scribbled notes and observations.

He was phenomenal. What they shared was. How was it possible for it to keep getting better, deeper, the fire raging higher?

It had to be the clock ticking. She'd heard that timed liaisons had a way of keeping the passion burning, every sensation exquisite, every feeling soul-shattering.

And she only had three weeks left. This time, when he left, it would be really all over. For her.

She tried to stifle the gutting dejection. She'd agreed to his rules. Ha. She'd snatched at any extension with him.

Live now! To the last moment.

She caught his eyes as she took the chart out of his hands and what she saw there…! Could it mean what she so insanely prayed and wept for? That he felt something for her beyond sexual dependency? That he might extend their liaison, at least keep the door open for future possibilities, sporadic reunions?

She couldn't hope for that. She'd better not!

She cleared the suffocating longing out of her throat and gestured towards Mr. Khurdi. "If you really want my diagnosis, I think he has a hydatid in his liver! OK, go ahead, laugh!" As he would, no doubt, if she told him how she loved him.

"Why should I when I think you're 100 per cent correct? When I'm impressed out of my mind that you actually thought of it?"

A hundred giant butterflies tried to burst out of her chest.

Don't make me love you any more. There is no more. I can't stand any more.

It was getting harder and harder not to tell him how she felt, not to scream her love in his arms as he transfigured her with ecstasy, or when he helped her and validated her and made her feel like the only woman in the world, the most precious human being in existence.

"I would really love to know how you came by the diagnosis. Give me a detailed performance of your beautiful mind at work, *amore.*"

She busied herself with placating Mr. Khurdi, answered Dante only when she got her erupting pulse under control. "Before I give you any performances, I want to know what you think we should do about it. My knowledge doesn't extend to knowing if it's operable or inoperable."

"From its location and his general condition, operable. Definitely. Do you have time to help me, *tesoro*?"

Oh, how she reveled in his precious professional faith. But she remembered something. She felt reluctant to convey it, but couldn't withhold it with a clear conscience. "Uh, Helena wanted to assist you some time. And I guess I can't hog you all the time."

"*Amore*, you still don't believe you have *carte blanche* to do anything you want with me? With my eternal gratitude? But, seriously, I don't want anyone else to assist me, if it's at all avoidable. If it's a must, just this time, let Helena be the second assistant."

"Uh, so what do I tell Mr. Khurdi? He's getting agitated."

"I can see that. OK, tell him he has a parasitic infestation by a tapeworm of the genus *Echinococcus granulosus* which is causing him a disease called cystic hydatidosis of the liver, the favorite target of the organism. At least one cyst now is over five centimeters in size and that's why its pressure produced symptoms of obstructive jaundice and abdominal pain. I also suspect he has bile sac rupture, therefore his classical triad of biliary colic, jaundice and urticaria."

She turned her back to the patient and shook with suppressed laughter. Dante widened his eyes in devilish innocence. "What? He should know all that!"

A splutter escaped. "I'm sure it would also interest him to know that the stuff he passed in vomit and stools was the hydatid membranes when the cyst ruptured!"

"Ah, so that is how you diagnosed it!"

"That, the triad and him living in a country in his childhood where it is endemic. He used to live in Greece."

"Brilliant, *bambola*! So, shall you tell him all that?"

She gave him an affectionate nudge. "Just tell me what I can tell him about the surgery."

"Tell him that's it's nothing serious now he's diagnosed. We'll take care of him, I'll just go in, remove the ruptured gall bladder, remove the parasite and sterilize the cyst cavity by injection of a scolicidal agent. Hmm, we do have formalin here, don't we?"

"Dante! You don't tell patients you're going to inject them with formalin!" She knew he was teasing her, knew how considerate he was with his patients.

He pretended bafflement. "It is what I'm going to do!"

"Well, I'll stick with telling him it's a solicidal agent—hell, a parasite killer. I'm not about to try to explain to him why we're going to inject him with something used in preserving corpses!"

In twenty minutes, the surgical team was gathered around the sedated Mr. Khurdi and Dante was taking one more look at the X-ray and ultrasounds.

He snorted in disgust.

Gulnar raised her eyes from her final preparations of the surgical instruments. "We already knew X-rays aren't well known for their reliability in detecting hydatids."

He rotated his neck, working a crick out. "I do wonder why we bother with X-rays at all. And ultrasound results remain operator-dependent."

Her eyes caressed him. "And since our operator is

the best there is, we did find confirming signs—daughter cysts, sand…''

''But not an exact position. But, wonder of wonders, there is the barest shadow in the X-ray of a thin rim of calcification delineating the cyst.''

''Enough for you to go in with confidence?''

He gave the X-rays one last assessing look, then handed them to her. ''I believe so.''

''OK, Dante, he's under. You can go ahead.''

Dante looked at his anesthetist. Sam Hiller wasn't looking at him. Not likely when he could barely take his eyes off Gulnar. Dante sympathized. And because he knew Gulnar was his alone, as long as their… arrangement lasted, he didn't mind.

He still couldn't believe what she'd done to him. She'd created new facets in him, new personas. The perpetually lusting male. The powerless, dependent creature. The devil-may-care rogue. The fearless fighter. And then there were the richness and tenderness and joy and freedom and constant surprises…

He knew he was heading fast for the fall of his life, the one he'd never recover from. He'd taken the leap into the chasm the day he'd come back, was now suspended in mid-air. Until he began his descent and crashed, it felt like soaring.

Helena's guttural voice intruded into his contemplations as he marked the field of surgery on Khurdi's abdomen. She was asking Gulnar something, her eyes as heavily on him as Sam's were on Gulnar. But that he minded. He shouldn't have agreed to make her his second assistant. Hell, he didn't need a second assistant.

He shook his head and decided to give the staring Helena something to do to take her focus off him. ''Gulnar, will you tell Helena to go find out if we have

0.5 per cent cetrimide solution in our pharmacy? It's the agent of choice for cyst cavity sterilization. If we have it, I'd rather use it instead of formalin.''

Gulnar translated and the woman at last shifted her glassy blue eyes off him and went out to do his bidding. He breathed a sigh of relief. Then he began the procedure.

He made a mid-line incision at the same level as the cyst, then deepened it throughout the layers of the abdominal wall then pulled back as Gulnar placed self-retaining retractors, opening the operative field.

''We need to protect the surrounding tissues,'' he informed her. ''Once I begin removal of the daughter cysts, any spillage can seed the abdomen with the parasite and cause secondary infestation.''

''As I remember—packing by formalin soaked packs?''

''You remember right.''

They finished packing the abdomen then he began evacuating cysts by strong suction and injecting formalin into their cavities. He repeated the procedure until the return was completely clear then instilled formalin into the cavities.

''We'll let it sit for ten minutes, evacuate it, irrigate the cavities with isotonic sodium chloride solution. This ensures both mechanical and chemical evacuation and destruction of all cyst contents.''

Helena came back at that moment, sniffed the formalin and frowned.

''Tell her we're sorry to send her on a wild-goose chase.'' He fixed his eyes on Sam's. ''That Sam remembered just after she left that we had none, so I went ahead and used the formalin.''

Sam didn't bat an eyelid. Dante knew Helena made

him uncomfortable, too. He played along, made apologetic gestures at Helena, said sorry in Badovnan.

"Would you like to fill the cavities?" Gulnar nodded eagerly. He made space for her to perform the task. After she was finished she stepped aside and Dante returned to his place.

"Reverse cutting needle? Vicryl absorbable sutures?" Gulnar asked. He nodded and she handed him the needle holder with the threaded needle to close the cysts with. "The main cyst looks too large a hole, Dante. Do you think we need a piece of omentum to fill it first?"

That was a really good idea—using a piece of the fatty sheath of the abdominal organs as filler. "Didn't think of that but, yeah, I should."

After he did that, he removed the ruptured bile sac, inspected the inside of the cyst, and sutured the opening where it communicated with the bile duct.

"Done. Sam?"

Sam looked at his monitors. "Strong and steady, like he's napping."

Dante yanked his mask down, stripped off his gloves. Gulnar shot him a questioning look. "You and Helena wrap up. Irrigate copiously with formalin then saline. And I mean copiously. Then, if she's very anxious to get some surgical practice, you guide her through closure." Her questioning look became one of extreme dismay. It seemed no one wanted anything to do with the buxom Helena.

He got up, giving her a you-got-her-here glance. On his way out she muttered, for his ears only, "You'll pay for this!"

He stopped, dropped his heated retort in her ear,

stopped himself with all he had from pushing her cap off and making a feast of it. "Any price, *amore. Any price.*"

The razor stroked down his nape. Dante squeezed his eyes tighter and surrendered to the incredible sensation. He was already addicted to this. Gulnar shaving him had to be the most erotic experience of his life. Right next to anything else he did with her. It was even more mind-melting now with them naked, just minutes after they'd made love. The feel of her lushness pressing his back, the feel of her hands spreading the gel foam, feathering his face and skull to adjust the angle she needed, her breath on him as she leaned in to concentrate on the harder-to-navigate areas around his ears, whispering to him how he'd felt inside her, how she craved everything they had together...

How would he ever shave his own head again? How would he ever even breathe, exist...?

"Can I ask you a question?"

His eyes snapped open. Gulnar hadn't been asking him any questions. She'd told him almost everything there was to know about herself. Her childhood, her experiences in war, her refugee years, her dead fiancé. She'd even cleared away his agony over her and Lorenzo. But she hadn't asked him anything in return. Sure, she asked just about everything that revealed his character and mind and preferences, just nothing that involved divulging personal data or facts from his past, none since asking about existing commitments. She hadn't even asked how or why his marriage had ended. It amazed him, her lack of curiosity.

Or was it her way of keeping him anonymous, making sure he ceased to exist for her once he was gone?

If so, it was as it should be. And it hurt.

But maybe she was going to ask now. Should he answer?

With his heart dropping beats, he barely articulated a rasped, "Go ahead."

Her hair spilled over his shoulder, caressing, scorching him with its heat and beauty. Then her question did. "Why do you keep your head wrapped up all the time?"

Ha. What a fool. Gulnar would never want to know any real information about him, would she?

Why should she when she already knows the only things that matter about you? a voice whispered inside him. *She's the only one who ever asked the right questions, the only relevant ones...*

He didn't want to dwell on this now. *Answer her.* "I want to be bald, but the world doesn't agree to my decision. Everyone stares and-or bombards me with questions. A scarf solves the problem. I have a shaved head beneath it and people don't see it to ask about it."

"They don't ask about the scarf, then?"

"It generates less interest. Seems I'm less conspicuous with it on."

Her nod was thoughtful. "It does detract from your shaved magnificence."

"Magnificence!"

"You do know how utterly breathtaking you look, bald?"

He'd thought it repelled her! At least at first. That first time when she'd seen him without the scarf. The shock in her eyes then—how could it still hurt, after all that time, and the thousand ways she'd shown him how much she lusted after each inch of him? He stood up, running his hands over the perfect smoothness she'd achieved. "First that I've heard it! I've been actually thinking of growing my hair back."

Her dimpled, flushed lips spread, indulgence incarnate. "Don't you dare! Haven't you ever looked in the mirror? In women's eyes?"

He went back to their mattress on the ground, stretched out, reached out his hand to her. "Haven't seen anything in either."

Her eager leap into his arms uprooted his heart all over again. "And in my eyes?"

Hunger. Appreciation. Constant and consuming. He saw that. Reveled in it. Lived for it. What would he live for after her?

For now, his hand trailed gratefully, proudly over her perfect buttock, up her satin, resilient back, ended up cupping her hungry breast. Her erect nipple hardened more. "Yeah, there I see things."

"What? Tell me."

"I see you and me, always ready, always hungry, feasting, worshiping. I hear us, I feel us, merged, sharing every intimacy, every privilege. Am I reading right?"

She came fully over him, rose to straddle him. He was hard again. Aching, maddened, as if he hadn't found total satisfaction inside her just minutes ago. As if he'd been aroused all his life without possibility of relief. She took him in her hands, rested him against her flat, firm belly, stroked him, stoked him. He thrust himself into her grasp. "Your sight is perfect—double meaning, oh, so intended. Now use it to watch this…"

She rose on her knees, and a little more besides to scale his length, rested him at the honeyed heat of her entrance. Holding his eyes, she opened on him. He lunged, tried to plunge himself inside her in one thrust.

She shook her head, her beloved hair an indignant flame. "Watch, darling—watch me taking you, watch yourself invading me…"

"Gulnar, mercy—I'll come in a second like that…"

"I will, too—as soon as I have you where you belong. Watch us, darling…"

She sank on him, her mindless moans melting into delirium, taking all of him, the impending tremors of her quake that always hurtled him into his own soul-wrenching release already milking his girth for maximum stimulation, for her, for him. He shouted with it. His enslavement. Her domination. "Gulnar, *amore mio*…"

She screamed his agony back to him. *"Dante!"* Her desperation jolted inside him as she rose to begin another stroke. He thrust up into her and she took him, snatched at his length and thickness with her muscles. Then the tidal wave crashed.

He bucked off the mattress, raising her in the air with him. She was no longer bearing down on him, open, abandoning all to his impalement, her convulsions around him wrenching every last bolt of pleasure from every last nerve. He jetted inside her until he felt he'd poured out his life essence inside her.

Still jerking with the electrocuting release, he snatched at her as she collapsed on top of him, her shudders resonating with his, their tears of deliverance mingling.

"Give me your lips, Gulnar…" he gasped, needing the emotional surrender to complete the carnal abandon.

She groped for his lips, fed him her life and passion, her moans sinking through to his soul. "Dante—Dante, I love you—love you—my love, so much. You're my life, darling, my life…"

The words sank slowly into his mind.

Had she really said…? Not "I love what you make me feel" or "I love what you do to me" but "I love you" and "You're my life"?

Endless moments later his shaking hand raised her face to him and her dazed eyes, sated and dissolving in tenderness, slowly filled with horror. Then emptied.

CHAPTER THIRTEEN

GULNAR'S lungs emptied of air. Her heart of blood.

What had she said?

Oh, God. She'd told him.

And if the shock in his eyes was anything to go by, she'd told him the last thing he wanted to hear.

She pushed herself off him, shaking. "Strike that off the record, OK?"

He tried to catch her back, take her into his arms again. "Gulnar…"

She disentangled herself and rolled off the mattress. "No, Dante. Don't say anything. I shouldn't have said that. It's none of your business what I feel."

He sat up, barked in incredulity. "None of my business!"

"No, it isn't. We have a deal and I'm honoring it. Remember when you told me you'd work with me, that you'd handle your desire if I didn't want an affair, that it would be your problem and not mine? Well, same thing here. Let's just forget it."

He was silent for a long moment. She tried to busy herself with anything, putting on her shirt, folding up their strewn clothes, removing the mess of their last hasty meal. His arms suddenly took her from the back and she jumped. She hadn't felt him move. Her body felt swollen, uncoordinated, torn between wanting to lean into him, to take all she could before the end that she could now taste came, and wanting to bolt, so ashamed of betraying herself, of compromising him.

He buried his face in her neck, in her hair, his voice dark, ragged. "Tell me you didn't mean it, *amore*. Tell me it was just something you said in the throes of satisfaction."

Suddenly she was angry. She tore at his arms and turned on him. "Why? So you'd feel better? I told you it has nothing to do with you. I shouldn't have told you, I'm so sorry I have, but I'm not going to lie now and say it isn't real. I *know* I'm not entitled to anything, but I'm entitled to my emotions." She thumped her chest, hard, to knock back the heart that was struggling to erupt from her chest.

Then she was suddenly scared. She needed more time with him. She had to reassure him, convince him that nothing would change. "I won't impose my emotions on you in any way, Dante, believe me. I've loved you from our first day, but did I burden you with my emotions? I'm sure I didn't. I have no expectations, Dante. None. We'll go on as before, I'll continue to be your lov—y-your…your sex partner and when you decide to leave I will still lie in bed and I won't say a word to ask you to stay."

"You wanted to ask me to stay then…?"

"Yes! But I didn't, and I won't. You're free, Dante. No strings. It is my pledge, too."

He stood there before her, naked and precious, the substance of her soul and her despair. His hoarse groan was the very sound of desperation too. *"But I don't want you to love me!"*

She'd known that. But hearing him say it, and this way… Her own anguish bled out of her, black and wet and corroding. "What is this? What's with you? What are you afraid of? That I'll pursue you or make demands or scandals? I don't even know where you come from.

I don't know if this is even your real name, and I don't want to know. I don't want anything. I have no use for anything. I will live here and I will die here and you won't hear from me or see me again after you leave. I wanted the remaining time with you, but if you find the idea of me as a person with emotions, and not just your temporary nymphomaniac, so disturbing, so repulsive, then I'll leave. Right now.''

She could no longer see anything through the tears. But she could hear. Nothing. No answer. No telling her she was wrong, or to stay, for now, to continue their two months. Oh, hell. He probably thought worse of her than anything she'd ever tortured herself with. Blind, she turned to gather her meager belongings, stumbled and fell flat on her face on the ground.

"Gulnar!" His shout broke over her, his hands snatched her up.

She struggled with all her strength, knocked his hands off her. "You don't want me to love you, fine! I hate you! Are you satisfied? I hate you because in a minute, with just one look, with one sentence you degraded me, made me feel more worthless—dirtier than even those who killed my folks and kept me alive to play with.'' A hysterical cackle ripped out of her at his panting, horror-struck expression. "Don't worry, Dr. Guerriero, I'm clean, if you're thinking in belated horror about all the unprotected sex we had. I'm also using birth control. You won't one day find a baby being pushed on you in your private clinic back in the States, a memento of your time here.''

Something erupted from him. It wasn't a sound. Just a terrible, devastating shock wave. It drove her to her knees. She rummaged after the articles she'd dropped, her hands useless. She was openly weeping now. "I know my place—my worth. I know m-my use. And I know I've…outlived it. I just hope you had some…fun. You'll have…no trouble finding a replacement for…the remainder of the two months. Women like me—desperate bodies to slake your lust in—are a dime a dozen in refugee camps. I wouldn't pick Helena, though. I think this is one…for fatal attraction scenarios."

Something huge and heavy landed just inches from her body. She wiped her eyes in fright and saw him. He'd fallen to his knees before her. And his face! Distorted beyond recognition, and— Oh, God, he was weeping, too!

All her agony was thrust aside, making way for his. She surged up, threw her arms around him, contained him in a quaking embrace. "Dante, no, don't—don't, darling. I didn't mean to upset you. I'm just a self-pitying fool and I didn't mean it. I'll never, never, never hate you. I'll love you till my last breath but I'll leave you alone, I won't give you any trouble. And don't feel bad about me, darling. You'll forget me soon, so just forget me now…"

He roared, harsh sobs shaking him and her around him. "Stop, stop, *stop*! Stop it, Gulnar, *stop it*. Oh, God, what did I do to make you feel this way? That's how you think I think? That my mind and soul are infested with all this ugliness? This narcissism and cruelty and exploitation?"

Her arms squeezed him tighter, pressing his face into her bosom, quailing. "No, no. It's me, it was my scars, my hang-ups talking, darling. I know you're the most noble human being, the most self-sacrificing. I didn't know someone like you could exist. It isn't your fault that you don't love me and I am not fit to love you.

You deserve someone whole and healthy in mind and psyche, and I'm—''

''*Shut up*, Gulnar,'' he thundered. ''Shut up! Are you totally insane? This is how you think of yourself? Can't you see what you are? You're everything that's worthwhile. Everything that's right and pure and human. Nothing is enough to do you justice. You're all that matters. You think I don't want you to love me—for me? I can't let you love me, for you. So you won't be hurt when I am no longer there...''

She smoothed her hands down his cheeks, every tear she wiped away scorching away her skin, abrading one more layer off her shredded heart. ''But I can't stop loving you. I thought I loved Evraim. I thought when he died that I couldn't risk loving again. But it took loving you to show me I knew nothing about love, that I can and will love, no matter what the risk. I will love you as long as I live because you're why I'm alive. I accept that you'll go, I won't ask for anything...''

''You will have everything I have to give. You already do. I just can't give you me. That is why I want you to stop, take back the heart you gave me, protect it.''

''I don't understand. I told you I accept you'll leave—''

''I won't leave. I'll *die*!''

Dante watched the effect of his words slashing across Gulnar's face and wished he'd never met her. Never loved her. She'd conquered war, she'd survived displacement and abuse, she'd outlived all her loved ones. Until he'd loved her. And destroyed her.

Her tears were now a steady stream. Were they changing color? Would they become the blood streaming out of his heart? He growled at the morbid thoughts, tried to disentangle himself from her clutching arms. This time they fell away, nerveless, powerless.

The sound that came out of her wasn't her voice. "What do you mean, you'll die?"

May as well tell her. She'd suffer for a while, then hope would die and she'd regain her will to live, separate from him. "I have cancer. Testicular. Third stage."

Her tears turned off. His did, too. This moment went beyond tears.

He was letting her down. Like everyone in her life who'd failed to protect her, and themselves.

He didn't know how long she sat there staring at him, her face frozen, breathless, pulseless, like him. Then she spoke, thick and slurred. "Cancer is treatable now."

He got off his knees, slumped against the tent wall. He was still naked, and he suddenly couldn't bear her eyes on him. Now she knew. He dragged the sheet over his lap. "I've had treatments. Six years ago, when I first discovered it."

Her sudden movement startled him. She surged from her kneeling position, erupted to her feet, came looming over him. "Will you tell me everything, or do I have to keep dragging it out of you?"

A goddess. This was what one had to look like. Standing there in only her unbuttoned khaki shirt, her beloved, lush body bathed in peach and agitation. He wanted to drag her on top of him, remove the sheet and bury himself in her. This was where he wanted it all to end. But he wouldn't do that to her.

"Sit down. It's a long story." He waited until she knelt in front of him again and looked her straight in the eye. "I once had it all—what society advertises as 'all' anyway. A rocketing career, a lot of money, accumulating offers, endless opportunities. And I had youth—and health, too. A surplus of it. I was thirty-five and was still competing in short-distance swimming championships— and winning.'' He saw realization in her eyes as they roved the expanse of his swimmer's shoulders and torso. He hadn't known what they'd been for until she'd rested her head there, pressed herself to his heart.

He ran agitated hands over them now, trying to put out the fire trails her gaze left behind. "I had patients flying me from all over the globe to perform the reconstructive surgery only I can perform. I had houses and estates in every country that took my fancy. I had an obscenely well-paid staff of twelve to organize my days for me. I had a glamorous wife who ornamented my bed, my many houses and public appearances. I had a mother who doted on me and four half-brothers and half-sisters who adored me. Then I felt a lump in my testis.''

Gulnar's face settled into the neutral mask she'd presented him with during her daily visits in hospital. Was she withdrawing? No, no—but, yes, for her sake, let her drift away, let the illusion of loving him fade. He didn't matter.

"My wife was scared witless, said she'd never noticed anything. Probably because we haven't been making love for over a month at a time, and when we did, she didn't do much...exploration.''

That got a response from Gulnar. She bit down on her lower lip—hard. Did she hate the idea of another woman's hands on him, even in the past, even when he was telling her how disappointing it had been? Only fair. He felt like killing anyone who'd ever touched her, without—or with—her consent. He exhaled the wave of blinding aggression, continued. "I went in for tests and, yes, I had a tumor, and it had already metastasized, everywhere."

An intake of trembling air was her only response. He went on. "Lungs, liver, bones. Before debating treatment options I had to have the radical inguinal orchidectomy to remove the testis and the abdominal lymph nodes and find out what kind of cancer I had." He could read what leapt into her mind. She'd had her hands all over him there, fondling, her lips suckling, and now her eyes followed, remembering… How ridiculous was it to get aroused while talking about the most emasculating experience a man could have?

He shook his head. "Phil, my friend and urosurgeon, unasked, decided to substitute what he removed with an artificial implant. Didn't want me to suffer body image problems. Didn't want my young, passionate wife to miss out on the feel of an even pair. Not that he thought such trivial things would rock our stable marriage." He huffed in sarcasm. "He also advised me for the sake of our future family to consider sperm cryopreservation, since permanent sterility was one of the possible outcomes of treatment."

Her lids lowered, then squeezed. Now she knew he hadn't been a careless, selfish bastard, making love to her without protection. "The tumor was a non-seminoma, the worst prognosis type at stage three. Everyone advised me to go all out with high-dose systemic chemotherapy, radiation and autologous bone-marrow transplantation. They removed bone marrow before chemotherapy, treated it with chemotherapeutic agents then froze it. After the chemotherapy infusions destroyed what remained of my bone marrow, they reinjected it into me.

"I had an almost fatal infection and after they resuscitated and stabilized me, they kept trying to vary the agents, the combinations, the dosages. Nothing seemed to be hitting me any less and the metastases were resistant. I went from two hundred and twenty pounds to one hundred and fifty in three months. I looked like a corpse and had the energy of one. I had originally decided to have my chemotherapy on an outpatient basis, but I was soon hospitalized. For six months. Until no metastases could be detected. During that time, I didn't want anyone to see me. I told my wife and family to just phone me."

The memory of those days made him restless. Not memories of the degradation of disease and incapacity, not the dread of a long, agonizing decline before the end, but of discovering the truth about his so-called loved ones, the people in whom he'd invested such presumptuous faith, so much life. He got up, yanked on his jeans. Gulnar's emerald eyes followed him, reddened, puffed, hanging on his every word.

"Roxanne…" He wouldn't keep calling her his wife. She'd never been his wife. Gulnar was. The one he'd pledged himself to. His only love. The one who'd inherit from him. He'd made all the plans. "Roxanne was horrified to see me the day I went home. She'd thought I'd be back to normal. She'd seen me once after I deteriorated and lost my hair and she'd thrown up then." He skimmed his hand over his smooth head. "If you're wondering. I couldn't bear my hair when it grew back, so I kept shaving it. She thought I was crazy to prefer being an 'egghead' to my previous glossy black haircut."

Gulnar's teeth made a curious sound. His lips quirked. "She couldn't bring herself to come near me.

When I assured her I wasn't contagious she was enraged. I wasn't painting her as a superficial flake. No woman in the world could bear seeing her husband looking like that. I excused her—really.''

Gulnar's eyes spewed forth wrath. She didn't, huh? His lips twisted again. ''Gulnar, in war zones, you see people mutilated, handicapped, emaciated, but a person ravaged by chemotherapy—it's all in the transformation—it was horrifying. You see me now, when I'm 80 per cent of my old self. She saw a zombie.''

Why was he defending Roxanne? He knew why with her next words. ''Are you trying to tell me I'd feel the same in her position? That this is the kind of horror you're trying to save me? Dante—besides loving *you*, I do love your body, I am addicted to its pleasures, and it would pulp me to see its beauty destroyed, its power extinguished. But my torment wouldn't be for me.''

And there was all the difference. Roxanne had thought only of herself. Gulnar thought only of him.

He couldn't let her do that. He wouldn't.

He heaved in a shuddering breath. ''Anyway, I told her my prognosis was fifty-fifty. I hadn't even told her that my sterility, if permanent, wouldn't mean we couldn't have children when she said she couldn't bear waiting for me to relapse. She decided it was time to also reveal that even when I was healthy I was a disappointing lover, and from then on my sex drive would diminish, even disappear. She'd been reading up on the subject.'' He huffed a chuckle now. What a load of bull. It was all about who. At his fittest, Roxanne had put out his fire. Now Gulnar had him constantly burning. She'd been his first real sex, too. ''In short, she wanted out.''

Gulnar's lips thinned, but she didn't say anything.

Her eyes said it all. He quirked her an indulgent smile. His virago. She'd defend him against everything. Even past injustices and injuries. And he believed she'd wipe them out, too. She already had.

"I gave her an instant divorce and half of my possessions in settlement. I went back to work and for a year and a half I went for follow-ups. The only finding was that the sterility was confirmed. Along the way I realized I was living someone else's life, doing it right only because I give everything my best. So I cut every professional tie and donated everything to charity. And it was then that I found out the rest of the truth.

"My mother, brothers and sisters turned on me like rabid animals, filed a dozen lawsuits against me to declare me incompetent, to take control of my fortune, when they got it back from the charities I'd donated it to. I left them to it, walked out. I stopped my follow-ups and pledged whatever time I had left to live to worthier pursuits, to taking chances, as extreme as need be, to achieve all the things others' expectations had stopped me from pursuing, to reach all the people who could have never afforded me in my previous fake life. And here I am."

Gulnar rose, came towards him, her eyes scorching him. "Yes, here you are. *Four* years later. Strong and healthy and beating the odds—conquering death even. If you're not back to normal, it's because you neglect yourself!"

"Gulnar, it's a matter of time before I relapse…"

"You don't know that!"

"I may have already relapsed, I just haven't been checking up to find out. I may have cancerous recurrences all over my body as we speak…"

"And you think I care? What's your worst-case scenario? That you won't last a year? I was trading my *life* for *two months* with you. What do you think I'd trade for *a year*?"

Too much. Too much. Love, gratitude, pride, agony, desperation. He staggered around, tears pummeling their way out of his very depths again. "No, no, *no*, Gulnar. I'm not putting you through this. And I'm selfish, too. I can't bear seeing anything but admiration and burning hunger in your eyes. I can't see worry and pity and anguish replace that. Dying is fine by me, it's torture I can't stand. You said so yourself during the hostage situation. I've been through every physical and psychological agony. And you know what? They're nothing compared to the month away from you, nothing compared to fearing for you on all counts. You may think you can bear it, seeing me fade away, but you won't. I can't—I *won't* do that to you!"

"Do you love me?"

Her tear-drenched, suffocating question splintered his agitation, silenced everything. He swung back to her, saw his devastation reflected in her every quivering facial muscle. "Love you? Love you? No, I don't love you, Gulnar…" She lurched as if he'd shot her, and he roared with it all. "I love cold days and cast skies, I love the night and children's laughter, I love an exhausting workout. I love cats and horses and dolphins. I love a couple of friends. I thought I loved my family. And, hell, yes, I love life and I love myself. You, *you*— I have no name for what I feel for you. It's all that I can feel, all that I never knew is there to feel. It's infinite and unconditional. It's blinding, agonizing, crippling, it's exquisite and illuminating and empowering. It's unadulterated ecstasy and pure torment—it's all there. It's everything. I'm only sorry it is so potent it made you love me.''

''You're sorry I'm *alive*?'' He jerked at her intensity then at her rough grab for him. He was already so shaky, he lost his balance. They went down together on the mattress. She kissed him, hard, then harder and harder, all over his face, her tears filling his eyes, his mouth, his soul. She expended her frenzy and slumped on him, her lips at his healed wound, her bleeding words filling his chest. ''I lived only when I loved you. Now I realize it's because you loved me, too. I don't care for survival any more. Either I live, and that's with you, or I don't.''

He went death still. Pain was flooding his left side. Was he having a massive coronary? Would he die of too much love, in her arms? He wasn't doing that to her either. ''No, Gulnar. No.'' His rasp was almost inaudible. ''You had the right idea all your life, not getting close so it wouldn't hurt to lose. I won't stay close so it will kill you to lose me. When I'm gone, you won't know what happens to me, may even hope I'm OK, and you'll always remember me as I am now.''

He tremblingly put her away and she clawed at him, weeping and wailing. ''The only thing that will kill me is losing you this way. Have mercy, Dante, don't leave me, not now that I know you love me, not this way…''

He jumped to his feet, grabbed his shirt, his backpack. He'd run. Run until he dropped. Then he'd lie there and let go. He'd just end this.

He escaped her snatching hands, long deaf so he wouldn't hear her wails, snapped the tent's zip down and ran out—and into six masked, armed men.

CHAPTER FOURTEEN

The men shoved him back into the tent, ramming him with the barrels of their guns. He shouted out the only thing screaming in his mind.

"Put something on, Gulnar, *now!*"

He struggled with them, giving her time to dress. In the end he stumbled back under their combined weight and violence, spilled from the inky night outside back into the light of their tent, glaringly artificial by comparison.

His gaze sought her. She'd slipped into her track pants, was now quakingly buttoning up her shirt. Their eyes collided, clung, communicated.

Don't worry. I'll be OK, his said.

I'm not worried. We're together, hers answered.

One of the masked men barked something Dante recognized as Badovnan.

"He's saying we're their prisoners. That they will avenge their brothers in arms," Gulnar whispered.

Dante laughed, loud and taunting. "How predictable."

The man barked again, at Gulnar. She said something, translated most probably. And the man turned on him, rammed him hard in his chest.

Dante gritted his teeth. "Gulnar, tell him, I'm the one who brought their terrorist operation down and caused the deaths of two dozen of their comrades."

Gulnar shook her head and he snarled, "*Tell* him, Gulnar."

She held his eyes for one more second then turned to the man. Her rapid Badovnan was cut short when the man swung the back of his hand and slapped her so hard she staggered and tumbled to the ground, sprawled flat on her back.

Dante's world exploded in vicious crimson. He heard a deafening roar and then he was straddling the man and bashing his head on the ground, the manic bellows unbroken. Then the world exploded again, in a detonation of blue and yellow. Then black.

Something fell on his cheek. He tried to brush it away and couldn't find his hands. He didn't care. Gulnar! Where was she?

He opened his eyes and she was there. It had been her tears that had roused him from unconsciousness. She was leaning over him, kissing him, whispering he didn't understand what. Then he did.

"Thank God— Oh, darling, are you OK?"

He didn't find his voice so he nodded. It took him another chaotic moment to realize. His hands were tied behind his back. Then it all came back.

He'd attacked the piece of trash who'd struck Gulnar down. He remembered his clear intention to kill the man. No one was abusing her ever again. He'd given it a good shot, too, until the bastard's comrades had come to his rescue. From the nauseating pounding in his head, and the fact that he'd been unconscious, they'd bashed him, and hard, on the head.

He struggled up to a sitting position, looked around.

Gulnar gave him specifics of their location. "It's one of their bases in the Badovnan mountains. We drove for seven hours."

He'd been out that long? He wondered if he'd have

any residual neurological damage. Didn't matter now. One thing did. Getting Gulnar out. To plan this, he had to have as many facts as possible. "Molokai?"

"Yes."

"I guess I should have expected it."

"I don't see why you should have. It wasn't very plausible for him to venture into the Sredna camp when it's heavily guarded by a multinational peace-keeping force."

"Not plausible, but apparently very possible, since we're here."

"They had plenty of help on the inside, people who made it possible for them to infiltrate and overpower security."

It figured. "The woman who confronted you the day you arrived?"

"And whomever she convinced to help. I guess it was too much to believe she'd set aside her hatred."

"The vindictive bitch! You personally saved her youngest child when she was dumb enough not to recognize he was having an anaphylactic reaction and not his usual asthma attack!"

Gulnar edged closer to him, rested her head on his shoulder. "I guess she hated me even more afterwards."

Outrage rushed to his head. "Sick. Just plain sick."

"But not surprising. You don't find a lot of balanced psyches in refugee camps, Dante."

"Don't make excuses for that bitch. You're what proves a pure soul remains so no matter what." Her eyes filled. He bent and closed each one with a hot, cherishing kiss. "Which is probably more reason for her to hate you." He straightened. They needed to use the minutes they had to themselves. "What more do you know?"

"Just that we're waiting for their boss to come, that he intends to make an example of us for the example we spoiled."

Hmm. Molokai himself was coming? He could use that.

And he would get his chance, right now. The door to their cell opened, and four armed men preceded a taller, more distinctive one. Molokai.

"Well, well, if it isn't our worthless host!" Dante took the offensive. He knew what kind of instinctive response he would get from Molokai. He made his blood boil. And one of the men present was Molokai's right-hand man. The one who understood good English.

Molokai just smirked. "Guerriero. We meet again."

"Yeah, fancy that. Still playing terrorist, Molokai, like the vicious, stupid failure that you are? Is this how you pretend to be a man? Play with big guns and attack only the unarmed? You want to make an example of me? How about you do it personally, you bed-wetter?"

Molokai's steel-gray eyes flared. Then froze again. "If you think you're going to anger me so I'll kill you right away, you're wrong."

Dante captured the eyes of Molokai's right-hand man, shoved his point home. "I'm *daring* you to show your men you can kill me without their help. You've made fools of them, sold them the lie that you're a man when you're just a dirty rat, that you're a hero when you're just an arms dealer making millions from their deaths and blind faith. I'm a surgeon, and I use my hands only to heal people. You're supposed to be a killer. Let's see who can actually—"

"*Shut up*, Guerriero. I should have killed you that

day you walked into my camp, asking to collect your debt!''

Good. He was already angry. On to the next step. ''You didn't only because I embarrassed you and your men were already restless about the siege in the municipal building. But you always kill those who help you, don't you? Like your brave men in the hostage situation? Do *you*...'' he swung his gaze to Molokai's right-hand man ''...know that Molokai sent your comrades to die? That he never intended to stage an attack to save them, that he intended to detonate the place with them inside? He's only angry his plan didn't work, that they didn't *all* die!''

Molokai took a few angry steps towards him, intending to kick him. Then he suddenly stopped and turned his soulless eyes to Gulnar. No. *Keep your attention with me, you bastard!*

Dante threw himself at his feet, bowled him over. Molokai landed with a heavy thud on the floor. Dante mounted him with his free legs and rammed him in his jaw with his head. In seconds he was hauled off him and the impacts of a dozen rifle butts were screaming down his nerves.

Molokai staggered to his feet, holding his jaw. ''Trying to turn my men against me won't work, Guerriero...''

''Oh, no?'' He turned to the men. ''Who do you believe? You kidnapped me from a refugee camp filled with your people, where I've been living in the tent you saw for yourself, to treat them, to save their lives. What does your leader do for these people? Or is he splitting his money with you and that's why you don't care?''

Gulnar suddenly spoke, translating, and from the amount she said it seemed it was everything he'd said from the beginning. He wanted to shut her up, made a desperate gesture for her to, but she shook her head and plowed on.

Molokai went for her and Dante roared, "Come near her and you will *die*, right now, Molokai! Do you hear me? You know I can do it. I brought your trained armed men down, alone and unarmed. I don't need my hands to snap your neck!"

Molokai stopped, his lips compressed. Gulnar kept talking. Then he smiled. "So she isn't just your harlot, huh? You care about her!"

Oh, God, no!

"That makes everything easier." Molokai rubbed his reddish beard. "You see, Guerriero, I want to put you on video, saying what I tell you to, begging and weeping for your life. I knew you might refuse to, even with torture. She'd do it, but I don't want a woman. Not good for our image. I want you! Now, if you don't, we'll rip her apart a piece at a time until you do!"

Dante's blood charred in apoplectic impotence. Gulnar said something to Molokai in Badovnan. His men gasped then a couple burst out in helpless snickers. She said more and two laughed outright.

Molokai snatched his gun from his holster and turned on her.

"Shut up, Gulnar!" Dante growled.

"Easy on the English, darling. The guys didn't understand a thing until I explained, and the one who understands English I think is with his boss on it. I think it was news to the others." Her eyes swung to Molokai. "Seems you're not that popular either, if they enjoy your embarrassment that much, Molokai."

Molokai bared his teeth. "Azeri bitch, I can shoot pieces off you and you'd still live. I don't need you in one piece to have your lover begging to do my bidding!''

Gulnar smirked. "Go ahead, you fart! Makes you more and more of the brainless, rattled coward that you are! So scared of a tied-up *woman*!" She quickly translated to the others, drawing more of their resentful glee.

"Gulnar!" Dante was losing his mind. He was still male and entitled to challenge Molokai to a degree, but her... Molokai might shoot her outright!

She turned flashing eyes on him. "I live with you, or not at all!"

No. *No way.*

Dante struggled to his feet. "Molokai! I'll do what you want. One condition. She walks out of here, gets delivered back to GAO, unharmed. I get proof of that, I'll record anything you want!"

"*No*, Dante. He'll double-cross you! He betrayed his own men and you think he'll honor his word to you, after you exposed him to his men?" She rushed to translate to the men.

Molokai gave her a murderous glance, circled around him. "How can I be sure you'd keep your word? You broke your word to me once."

Dante almost gagged on rage and loathing. "I didn't give you my word then. You allowed me two lives, didn't ask me to pledge my agreement. This time I am giving you my word."

The men's murmuring rose at Gulnar's translation and Molokai's almost colorless eyes crinkled. He was enjoying this, the son of a bitch! He said something to his men. They fidgeted.

They were hesitating to obey him!

Yes, *yes*! Their plan was working.

One of the men said something. Gulnar translated. "He's asking him if what we said is true."

Molokai turned on his man, fury blotching his pale complexion. Gulnar kept talking, addressing the other men. "I'm telling them their turn is coming, that he will just keep conning them, disposing of them one by one and getting more stupid recruits all the time, using their heroic example."

Molokai turned the gun on her and one of his men stayed his hand, raised his voice. The enraged exchange went over Dante's head. He only knew the tide was turning. He noticed the right-hand man slipping out. Then all hell broke loose.

There was a gunshot. A thunderclap, curdling Dante's blood. His shouts for Gulnar to get down were drowned in more and more gunshots and roars. Then a fully fledged storm of gunfire broke out—outside.

A man, bloody and inert, fell over Dante. He struggled to shove the body off him, bellowing for Gulnar to stay down, to answer him. He was heaving in a breath to bellow another shout when everything hushed. For five seconds. Then the door to their cell exploded open and a dozen heavily armed soldiers stormed in.

Dante barely registered them, his eyes seeing only to find Gulnar, his breath coming only to gasp an incoherent litany of her name. Then he found her. Face down, with one of the fallen men on top of her.

Hands were on him, someone was cutting his restraints and he was roaring for her. He exploded from the hands that pulled him to his feet, hauled the man off her and hurled himself to the ground beside her. She was covered in blood, unmoving. Air screamed in his chest, came out in choppy howls, his hands, out of control, groped for her pulse. Nothing. *Nothing.*

"Gulnar!"

Someone tried to help him turn her over. "No!" He rammed him away. No one was touching her. He'd do everything. He'd save her. He'd stop her hemorrhage and she'd be OK. *Get yourself together!*

"An emergency bag, *right now*!" he bellowed again, and the man who'd been trying to help sprang to his feet and ran out.

Forcing his hands to steady, Dante wiped his tears away, their flow only thickening as he turned her with all the care and the desperation that had long ruptured his heart. He had to hang on, for her. He'd give her every drop of his blood. And what if it wasn't enough...?

No! She *had* to live. He had it all planned. Her safe new life.

He checked her, murmuring to her. "Gulnar, *amore mio, ti amo, ti amo.* Open your eyes for me, darling." Where had the bullet hit her? Where had this blood come from? Her head, her chest, her abdomen, her back—nothing anywhere. So where? *Where?*

He should have taken her away sooner! He shouldn't have left her living as she had been one more day! He was to blame for this. He'd made an enemy of Molokai. He'd kept her near him, made her a target, too. But his greatest crime was that he'd been about to leave her, desolate and broken. She'd begged him not to leave her. Oh, God...

"Gulnar, *amore*, I won't ever leave you, never waste a moment we can spend together... Just open your eyes—I beg you!"

The emergency bag landed beside him. He didn't even notice who'd brought it. He tore it open, produced a stethoscope. But he was weeping now, huge racking sobs shaking him apart, and he couldn't hear a thing. He forced himself under control and smoothed her hair away, traced her closed lids, coaxed her flaccid lips apart, bent and breathed his whole life into them.

Her lips moved beneath his and his heart stopped. He jerked back to look at her and her eyes shot open, then she shot up to a sitting position, spluttering. He almost blacked out.

She swayed, too, slumped back, holding her head. "Molokai…he shot his man—he fell on me. I barely turned my face away before hitting the ground…" Her eyes focused on his distorting face and panic flooded them. "Dante, darling—what happened? Are you hurt?"

"Are *you*? I can't find any wounds and there is so much blood…" His words choked, his hands feverish all over her, his tears running faster.

"It has to be that guy's. I only hit my head— again…" He immediately pounced, examining her head, revisited nightmares of their first day, of fractures and accumulating intracranial bleeding robbing him of all reason. She caught at his hands, brought him down to her, rubbing her face against his. His buried his face into hers harder. He'd never, never let go. At least until… She groaned and he jackknifed up. "I'm OK. I know I am. It's just I have a wrecking ball inside my head. I always end up hitting the ground head first. Seems my head is the heaviest part of me!"

"And since it's also the toughest part of you, we shouldn't worry."

Both Dante and Gulnar blinked and swung their heads towards the speaker. Emilio!

"You both OK, then?" Emilio lips were tilted into a half-smile. His eyes were anything but humorous. Both

Dante and Gulnar, still clinging to each other, nodded mutely at him. "That was too close, folks. If it weren't for the info we got from Helena, we would never have found you. Yeah, your instincts about her were correct, Dante. She's Molokai's mole and she worked with Tatiana to distract the guards at the camp's access point near our tents. There were many casualties."

"Damn! *Damn*!" Dante snarled. "I should have heeded my instincts. And GAO should—must have—a better screening system for its recruits."

They were silent for a moment. Then Gulnar moved. Dante swooped to support her within the curve of his body. She chewed her flushed lip thoughtfully. "How did you find her out?"

Emilio pursed his lips, his face grim. "She seemed agitated after the attack and your disappearance became known. Her agitation felt disproportionate to her attachment to either of you and I got suspicious. I…persuaded her to talk. She was distraught that they took you, too. It was why she was so agitated in the first place. You're her precious Dr. Guerriero!"

Dante's stomach heaved. Gulnar ran a loving hand over his cheek, his head. "So she was getting rid of the competition, huh? I was right about the fatal attraction scenario, then. See what you do to women, Dante? She was willing to kill for you."

"One more word out of either of you…" Dante shredded the words and spat them out. "And I'm liable to break the woman's neck on sight!"

Emilio shook his head. "You won't see her. She's been taken into custody by the Badovnan authorities."

"Lucky her." Dante stood up, scooping Gulnar in his arms. "Let's get out of here."

Emilio closed the emergency bag, jumped to his feet. "You never said anything I liked better, Guerriero."

Four soldiers immediately flanked them as they came out of the room, escorted them outside where the rebel installation was being turned upside down and everyone was in custody. And there was Molokai, on a stretcher.

"Is he dead?" Gulnar asked.

Emilio snorted in disgust. "He isn't even seriously injured."

"I'll have a word with him," Dante snarled.

"Dante—let it go, my love."

He gave her lips a fierce press. "Stay with Emilio, *amore*. I'll be a minute."

She lowered her eyes, accepting his decision. His priceless Gulnar, giving him total freedom, when she knew one more word would have bent him to her will.

He approached the man who'd caused so much death and destruction, a bloody, flimsy body that housed a twisted and even flimsier soul. Molokai talked first. "How did you know?"

"About the remote-controlled detonation? You mean you don't remember that you bragged, like the insecure nothing that you are? As for knowing that your men didn't know how you were using them, that's what small, sick creatures like you always do."

"This isn't the end, Guerriero," Molokai rasped.

Dante shrugged. "It never is. But it is for you. I doubt you'll make it out of prison. Your fellow Badovnans are on to you now. Good riddance, Molokai."

Before the man said anything else, Dante had already deleted him from his mind, turned to Gulnar. Only she mattered.

She threw herself into his arms. He crushed her to him, every insupportable alternate scenario, all the things that could have gone wrong, polluting his soul, crushing down on his sanity.

But she was all right. She was alive and well and he'd make sure she was never in danger again. He had to get her out of here. Out of this region. Out of this lifestyle.

Eight hours later they were lying in bed in a hotel room in Zvetnia, Badovna's new official capital. They'd stumbled into the shower as soon as they'd entered, made desperate, ferocious love there, then again in bed, longer, tender and far more devastating. They now caressed and murmured and moaned their relief and their love.

Then Gulnar was getting out of bed. Dante clung to her. With a lingering kiss, she disentangled herself gently and headed for the bathroom.

Dante waited for her to come back, his whole being throbbing in impatience. She finally came out—dressed.

He jackknifed in bed. "Gulnar, where do you think you're going?"

She didn't meet his eyes, bent to the backpack Emilio had gotten her, checked her papers, her money. "Back to GAO's office in Srajna to reschedule my reassignment."

He didn't even feel himself move, just found himself in front of her, his arms hauling her to him. "You're not staying here at all, Gulnar. You're coming with me to the States."

She looked at him now, eyes wide, startled. "You mean...you changed your mind?"

He enfolded her in a shuddering embrace. "When I thought I'd lost you, I would have sold my soul a hundred times over for one more breath, and damned myself to hell for the way I was going to throw away the time we could have together. You were right. May God forgive me, but I can't end it now…''

Her shutters slammed down again, all her animation snuffed in a second. ''You mean you will—later?''

''We have to be sensible about this, *amore*. I want you with me until…''

She pushed out of his arms, her emerald eyes, the windows of her rich soul, blank. ''Until you relapse? Is that your plan? Then I'm supposed to desert you?''

He spread his arms, agitated. He had to make her agree to this. ''You won't be deserting me. It's what I'd want you to do!''

She tilted her head at him. ''Will you promise to leave me, too, if I get sick or crippled? This has to be a two-way deal, you know?''

''Don't be ridiculous…''

''Don't *you*! You're alive and healthy six years after having cancer diagnosed. I'd say your chances aren't any worse than mine of contracting a debilitating illness or getting maimed in an accident.''

''Don't say that!''

Suddenly she shrugged and her eyes— What was that he saw there? He didn't understand it, and it frightened him more than anything. ''And, anyway, even if we settle this, I always realized I can't be with you. Here we were just a man and a woman, but in your home I'll be what I really am and you'll be what you really are.''

This was what he'd instinctively dreaded. He saw where she was leading and he was damned if he'd let her go there. ''You're the woman I love, *my woman*. I'm *nothing* but your man.''

''We're both so much more that just that, Dante. I'm the scarred refugee, the product of a lifetime in war zones. You're the celebrated surgeon, the product of a stable life and society. You had a crisis, you fought your way out of it and now you're ready to resume your life. I never wanted you to love me like I love you…''

"I love you more—*more*, Gulnar. I told you how I love you. I'll dare death—and life—only if you let me love you.''

"Then love me, and come back whenever you can. I'll be always here, waiting for you.''

"I'm taking you out of here. You're never going to suffer or fear again.''

"What if I don't know how to live in safety, in normality?''

He reached for her again. He had to stop this, end it. "Don't be silly!''

She evaded him. "What happens if I don't fit into your life? If you find out that what you feel for me is a combination of your personal despondency and the traumatic circumstances? The heightened emotions, the sharpened desires…''

"Would *your* feelings change if you lived away from danger? Would you love me less, need me less?''

She shook her head, bent to pick her backpack.

He caught her back in trembling arms. "Then *don't* live with me! I'd planned it this way, originally. Those thirty-four days I stayed away? I went back to the States and arranged everything. I liquidated my assets and donated everything before I started wandering. But I had long-shot investments, shares in obscure projects that have become household names in the last four years. I sold my shares and put the money in the bank in your name. It's a lot. I left instructions with my attorney to come for you after I'd left, to take you home and do everything for you. The only difference now is that I will stay in your life, in any sort of arrangement that works for you.''

''Until you tell me it's over? Or will I tell you? When I find me some healthy American and hook up with him?''

The very idea. His damned imagination. It was beyond agony. He squeezed his eyes, his arms convulsing around her. *''Don't.''*

She squirmed against him, her voice thickening, drowning in anguish and tears. ''Don't what, Dante? Don't show you how preposterous your proposition is?''

He buried his face in her neck, shook with the enormity of it all. ''Gulnar—Gulnar—I can't let you suffer ever again. Never on my account.''

She turned her face into his, scalding him with her tears, the rawness of her voice, of her torment. ''Strange way you have of doing that, by slashing me to pieces.''

''And you're doing the same to me, insisting on remaining here!'' he choked.

''Just another way of showing you how it feels to be stymied by a totally moronic piece of roundabout, destructive logic.''

''You mean…?''

''Yes, I mean!'' She struggled out of his arms, turned on him, her eyes blazing. ''I was teaching you a lesson. Making my point. I can only give you up if you don't want me. But you do, and I'll do anything—put up with anything—to fit in your world, to keep on deserving your love. I don't care if I will be an outcast or whatever. I'll be with you and I'll do whatever is needed to remain with you. And whatever it is I have to do, it will be an honor and a privilege. *And* a pleasure. Not deserving you, losing your love and not fitting into your life are my fears, and that's what I intend to do about them to be with you. I've long conquered my fear of losing your love. What will you do about your fears? How far will you go, how much will you endure to be with me?''

She reached for him, contained him in the only home he'd ever known, ever wanted. "I've loved a man who'd lost both his legs to the hip joint and there was only gratitude—happiness that he'd survived, that I was granted that extra time with him. There was no shadow of anguish or sacrifice then. Yes, beautiful, gentle Evraim. I left the refugee camp, I mourned and built my walls only when he died. Him, I loved. *You're* my life, and beyond. So let what we have ward off everything, fear and doubt and illness. Let me be yours, for better or for worse.''

He pulled back, looked down at her and saw conviction to conquer fate, love to change destiny in her determined, streaming eyes. He knew then. He'd be with her to his dying day. And that day wasn't coming any time soon. He'd make sure of it.

He bent and scooped her up. He placed her on the bed, loomed over her. He spread her arms, threaded their fingers and their gazes. "You want to know how far I'll go? What I'll endure? I'll go as far as ninety and I'll endure everything I've endured times a thousand. And I'll be the happiest man in creation, doing it all. If you'll take me, let me be yours, for better or for worse.''

She suddenly grabbed him, brought him on top of her, sank her lips in his. "I'll take you, my heart, any way at all. Now, show me some better…''

His surprised chuckle erupted at her sudden change from super-charged emotion to all-out seduction. Her clothes dissolved in his hands. Then as he joined them, took them both home, he groaned to her, "I'll show you better—*and* better. Cry out when I'm doing it right…"

She cried out all night.

1005/03a

MILLS & BOON®

Live the emotion

_Medical
romance™

THE NURSE'S CHRISTMAS WISH
by Sarah Morgan

Christmas is coming – but for A&E Consultant Mac
Sullivan it's just another day. Enter Nurse Louisa
Young, who brings warmth, sparkle and Christmas
into his department – can she bring it into his life as
well…?

*The Cornish Consultants: Dedicated doctors by day…
playboy lovers by night!*

THE CONSULTANT'S CHRISTMAS
PROPOSAL by Kate Hardy

Consultant Toby Barker has a secret: he has been in
love with Dr Saskia Haywood for years. Saskia also
has a secret: the illness she struggles with may mean
she can never have children. Both secrets are out
– but what Saskia doesn't realise is that Toby will do
anything for her…

NURSE IN A MILLION by Jennifer Taylor

The longer Dr Michael Rafferty spends trying to
persuade Nurse Natalie Palmer to return to the
Worlds Together team, the more he wonders why
he ever let her go from his life… But Natalie's
wealthy background makes him feel they are worlds
apart – can he look beyond it to happiness?

*WORLDS TOGETHER: A special medical aid team.
Love – and medicine – that knows no boundaries*

On sale 4th November 2005

*Available at most branches of WHSmith, Tesco, ASDA,
Borders, Eason, Sainsbury's and most bookshops*

Visit www.millsandboon.co.uk

MILLS & BOON®

Live the emotion

1005/03b

_Medical
romance™

A CHILD TO CALL HER OWN *by Gill Sanderson*

Dr Tom Ramsey is enchanted by the clinic's new midwife – she rekindles emotions Tom thought he'd never feel again. But midwife Maria Wyatt is haunted by memories – memories that come flooding back when she meets Tom's adorable son James…

DELL OWEN MATERNITY: Midwives, doctors, babies – at the heart of a Liverpool hospital

COMING HOME FOR CHRISTMAS
by Meredith Webber

A&E specialist Nash McLaren has come home for Christmas, and is surprised to hear GP Ella Marsden is back. He thought no one in the town would trust a Marsden again. But, working with Ella, Nash starts to remember how good it feels to be with her…

EMERGENCY AT PELICAN BEACH
by Emily Forbes

Dr Tom Edwards has come to Pelican Beach to escape city life – meeting Dr Lexi Patterson after five years wasn't part of his plan! But, working together, they save lives, share memories and become close. The career-driven Lexi of the past has changed – she can't let Tom go again…

Don't miss out!
On sale 4th November 2005

Available at most branches of WHSmith, Tesco, ASDA, Borders, Eason, Sainsbury's and most bookshops

Visit www.millsandboon.co.uk

researching the cure

The facts you need to know:

- **One woman in nine** in the United Kingdom will develop breast cancer during her lifetime.

- Each year **40,700** women are newly diagnosed with breast cancer and around **12,800** women will die from the disease. However, survival rates are improving, with on average 77 per cent of women still alive five years later.

- **Men can also suffer from breast cancer**, although currently they make up less than one per cent of all new cases of the disease.

Britain has one of the highest breast cancer death rates in the world. Breast Cancer Campaign wants to understand why and do something about it. Statistics cannot begin to describe the impact that breast cancer has on the lives of those women who are affected by it and on their families and friends.

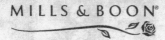

4 FREE

BOOKS AND A SURPRISE GIFT!

We would like to take this opportunity to thank you for reading this Mills & Boon® book by offering you the chance to take FOUR more specially selected titles from the Medical Romance™ series absolutely FREE! We're also making this offer to introduce you to the benefits of the Reader Service™—

- ★ FREE home delivery
- ★ FREE gifts and competitions
- ★ FREE monthly Newsletter
- ★ Exclusive Reader Service offers
- ★ Books available before they're in the shops

Accepting these FREE books and gift places you under no obligation to buy, you may cancel at any time, even after receiving your free shipment. Simply complete your details below and return the entire page to the address below. You don't even need a stamp!

YES! Please send me 4 free Medical Romance books and a surprise gift. I understand that unless you hear from me, I will receive 6 superb new titles every month for just £2.75 each, postage and packing free. I am under no obligation to purchase any books and may cancel my subscription at any time. The free books and gift will be mine to keep in any case.

M5ZED

Ms/Mrs/Miss/Mr ....Initials ....

BLOCK CAPITALS PLEASE

Surname ....

Address ....

....

....Postcode..

Send this whole page to:
UK: FREEPOST CN81, Croydon, CR9 3WZ